"YOU'RE A STRANGER HERE IN LOST SOUL . . . "

"Don't go makin' waves or you'll regret it. We got strict laws here." The marshal's eyes dropped to the worn butt of Slocum's six-shooter. "Nobody wears guns in town."

"I'll take it off later," Slocum said. "You ought to post your laws where a stranger can read them."

"No need. Everyone knows them," the marshal said. "Hand over that smoke wagon." He thrust out a meaty hand, waiting for Slocum to meekly surrender his six-shooter.

"Reckon that's not going to happen, Marshal." Slocum didn't make a move toward the gun, but he didn't have to. He was fast, damned fast, and it showed in his stance. If the marshal tried to grab the gun or otherwise take it from him, there'd be a dead lawman on the sawdust-covered floor of the Prairie Dog Saloon. . . .

D1707458

DON'T MISS THESE
ALL-ACTION WESTERN SERIES
FROM THE BERKLEY PUBLISHING GROUP

THE GUNSMITH by J. R. Roberts
Clint Adams was a legend among lawmen, outlaws, and ladies.
They called him . . . the Gunsmith.

LONGARM by Tabor Evans
The popular long-running series about U.S. Deputy Marshal
Long—his life, his loves, his fight for justice.

SLOCUM by Jake Logan
Today's longest-running action Western. John Slocum rides
a deadly trail of hot blood and cold steel.

BUSHWHACKERS by B. J. Lanagan
An action-packed series by the creators of Longarm! The
rousing adventures of the most brutal gang of cutthroats ever
assembled—Quantrill's Raiders.

DIAMONDBACK by Guy Brewer
Dex Yancey is Diamondback, a southern gentleman turned
con man when his brother cheats him out of the family fortune. Ladies love him. Gamblers hate him. But nobody pulls
one over on Dex . . .

WILDGUN by Jack Hanson
Will Barlow's continuing search for his daughter, kidnapped
by the Blackfeet Indians who slaughtered the rest of his
family.

JAKE LOGAN

SLOCUM AND THE UNDERTAKER

J

JOVE BOOKS, NEW YORK

SLOCUM AND THE UNDERTAKER

A Jove Book / published by arrangement with
the author

PRINTING HISTORY
Jove edition / May 2000

All rights reserved.
Copyright © 2000 by Penguin Putnam Inc.
This book may not be reproduced in whole or part,
by mimeograph or any other means, without permission.
For information address: The Berkley Publishing Group,
a division of Penguin Putnam Inc.,
375 Hudson Street, New York, New York 10014.

The Penguin Putnam Inc. World Wide Web site address is
http://www.penguinputnam.com

ISBN: 0-515-12807-4

A JOVE BOOK®
Jove Books are published by The Berkley Publishing Group,
a division of Penguin Putnam Inc.,
375 Hudson Street, New York, New York 10014.
JOVE and the "J" design
are trademarks belonging to Penguin Putnam Inc.

PRINTED IN THE UNITED STATES OF AMERICA

10 9 8 7 6 5 4 3 2 1

SLOCUM AND THE UNDERTAKER

1

John Slocum wiped a river of sweat from his forehead using his dusty red bandanna. As he pushed back his Stetson, he looked into the clear, mercilessly bright blue Nevada sky. The summer sun beat down with a vengeance, but Slocum felt a thrill of anticipation when he saw the slow feathered circle of buzzards spiral lower in the distance. They had spotted something in the desert—and he hoped he knew what it was.

"Come on," he said to his tired horse. "We only have a couple more miles to travel. Then he's ours, one way or the other."

Slocum had been on Silas Baker's trail for more than two weeks, following him late one night from outside a Virginia City dance hall into this heat-racked cemetery of a desert. Baker had crept up behind Slocum while he was relieving himself against the saloon wall, slugged him, and stolen his winnings. It might have been that Baker was just a poor loser at cards. Slocum could understand that, even if he didn't appreciate what the man had done to him. But Baker was something more than a sneak thief. He had not been content to simply slug Slocum and steal his poker winnings.

After Slocum lay stretched out in the alley behind the

Fancy Lady Dance Hall, Silas Baker had fired a derringer twice at Slocum's back.

Memory of the backshooting rankled. Slocum stretched tight muscles, mopped up more sweat, and dismounted, leading his exhausted mount. He wanted to be there when the buzzards began picking the flesh off Baker's worthless carcass. And if Baker wasn't quite carrion for the buzzards, Slocum would remedy that with the speed of a bullet. He would not make the son of a bitch's mistake of firing into a wood plank instead of the man's back. It had been darker than the bottom of a well that night and Baker had been a little drunk.

Slocum was sober, and would have the pleasure of watching Baker die in the bright noonday sun.

"Just a mile more," he promised his horse. The mare neighed and shook her head, as if saying she wouldn't go one more step. But she did. She had heart. She might even appreciate the way Slocum walked alongside her rather than riding when victory was so close.

Slocum touched the ebony butt of his Colt Navy slung in its cross-draw holster. He was ready to bring some justice to Silas Baker. A noose might have been more appropriate, but Slocum considered a bullet faster punishment. An eye for an eye. Baker had tried to shoot him. Slocum would return the favor, but he'd make sure Baker saw death coming and knew who fired the slug that ended his putrid life.

Topping a sunbaked ridge, Slocum stared down into a mile-wide sandy bowl, shielding his eyes against the pitiless sun. What he saw wasn't what he expected. Someone was in big trouble, but it wasn't his quarry.

"Damn," Slocum muttered. He had not been thrown off Baker's trail. It simply crossed that of a wagon train, apparently made up of tenderfoots and romantics.

No one else would be traveling in the middle of the day. No reputable wagon master would have brought his wards out onto this alkali flat, and no one with any sense would have riled the Arapahos to the point that they left their tepees and came after them in this heat. Slocum wiped away more sweat, then took a long drink from his canteen as he watched the deadly drama unfold in front of him.

The buzzards spiraled down lower, anticipating an easy meal as the Indians attacked with methodical skill. The Arapahos rode closer, fired a few arrows, then darted away, whooping and shrieking. Whoever was in charge of the thin line of wagons didn't have the sense to stop and fight. As a result, the Indians picked off the wagons one by one, starting at the rear and working forward. Already, two wagons had been set on fire, their drivers and passengers facedown on the sunbaked desert waiting to be scalped before the aerial carrion eaters had their fill.

It was not Slocum's fight. He had Silas Baker to track down, and evidence showed the man had kept moving toward a purple-shrouded mountain range on the far side of this hellhole of a Nevada desert. The mountains promised cool ponds of water and shade and possibly relief from the heat melting his bones.

Shade would have been enough of an attraction for Slocum, even if revenge wasn't dealt into the game. The wagon train wasn't his worry. He ought to wait for the Arapahos to finish them off, then move on and tend to his business with Baker.

He ought to do that. Slocum heaved a sigh, hitched up his gunbelt, and then drew the Winchester from its saddle scabbard. Letting ignorant sodbusters die wasn't in him. He had no quarrel with the Arapahos and seldom heard of them raiding these days. But he could not let the women and children suffer for the stupidity of their leaders.

Slocum snorted, settled down on the ground, and sighted along the barrel of his rifle. His finger came back smoothly, easily. The accurate shot took one Aarpaho from horseback. For a moment, the other Arapahos never noticed. Then Slocum shot another, winging the one he took to be the war chief. Feathers scattered as the slug ripped through a war bonnet and the chief swung around, gripping his wounded left shoulder.

The chief shouted and waved wildly, getting his braves assembled for a concerted attack on the only source of resistance.

Slocum sighed heavily. He had diverted the attack. Now he was on the receiving end of the Arapahos' vengeance. Slocum kept firing until the magazine emptied. He did not rush as he shoved one .44 cartridge after another into the magazine of the Winchester. His deliberate actions were born of long battles fought during the war, when his skill as a sniper had won more than one battle for the Confederate forces. Slocum had bided his time, waited for the flash of sunlight on a Union officer's braid, then fired. That same patience and calmness in the face of danger saved him now.

He emptied a second magazine, knocking another Arapaho from horseback. As he reloaded, the war chief reached the foot of the ridge where he had begun his one-man attack. The chief's wound bled profusely, and he wobbled as he waved his war lance in Slocum's direction.

Seeing he had no time to finish reloading, Slocum laid down his rifle and drew his Colt Navy. As the Arapaho chief charged uphill, Slocum cocked his six-shooter and waited for the warrior to come into range.

The first shot missed. So did the second. The third and fourth killed the Arapaho war chief. The riderless horse galloped past Slocum and allowed him to see that the rest of the braves were bearing down on him.

Slocum returned to loading his Winchester, then began firing. Someone among the surviving warriors took charge and halted the attack. Slocum stopped firing, waiting to see what would happen. If they tried following their chief up the hill, Slocum wanted them to join him wandering endlessly in the Happy Hunting Ground. The Arapahos milled around at the base of the ridge, then let out a whoop and trotted away.

He heard their insults and ignored them. Whatever it took

for the warriors to break off the attack and still think of themselves as valiant men was fine with him. He considered how much he wanted Silas Baker in his sights—and how little he cared to kill the Indians.

Slocum shoved his rifle back into its saddle sheath, then mounted and rode slowly downhill, his horse's hooves kicking loose stones and sliding a few times. Then he was on the alkali flat and riding toward the wagons, which were still making their way deeper into the hottest part of the desert.

He was worried the travelers might attack him, but more than one of the drivers had spotted him making his stand against the Arapahos. They actually reined back and brought their oxen to a halt so he could overtake them without chasing them into California.

"You all right?" Slocum shouted, not wanting some settler with an itchy finger to open up on him with a shotgun. He waited until a man walked out, a rifle held in the crook of his left arm. Slocum rode forward, then dismounted and met the man some distance from the last wagon in the train.

The last one that had been attacked directly. Slocum saw burned patches in the taut canvas. For some reason, the Arapahos' fire arrows had not taken hold and burned the wagon down to its frame as had happened with the other two.

"Who are you?" the man demanded.

"The son of a bitch that pulled your fat out of the fire, that's who," Slocum said angrily. He was in no mood to put up with the other man's suspicions. "If you hadn't been left out in the sun to have your brains cooked, you'd know I just saved your hide."

"Thanks," the man said. His attitude didn't much change. Slocum couldn't figure out the man's dog-in-the-manger demeanor.

Slocum hoped they all rotted in hell. He had risked his scalp to save them, and even the offer of a drink of water wasn't forthcoming.

"Keep going that way and you'll run out of water inside a day. That or your oxen will keel over on you," Slocum said. He turned, with an uneasy feeling that the man might just shoot him. With a loud protest from his horse, Slocum mounted and turned back toward Baker's trail. The fugitive had headed in the direction the wagon train had come from.

"Wait a minute," the man said. Slocum looked from him to the distant wagons. A half-dozen children peered out from the relative safety of their wagons at him. They all ducked for cover like rabbits hunted by a coyote when they knew he had spotted them.

"What is it?" Slocum asked, doubting the man was going to thank him for his help.

"You ride that way, you run into more of them heathens."

"Thanks for the warning," Slocum said, not bothering to keep the sarcasm from his voice.

"I mean it. We only rode past the canyon leading to the Valley of Spirits, nothing more. Those savages come boiling out and attacked us."

"Valley of Spirits?"

The man shuddered and gripped his rifle a tad harder. He nodded as if his head had been detached from his body and put on a spring. Slocum saw this was about all the thanks he was going to get—an odd warning that meant nothing.

He had started to ride on when the man called to him. "Wait. We want to thank you for what you done."

"Don't hurt yourselves none," Slocum said.

"Water!" the man said, a desperate note in his voice. "We can give you and your horse water! We got barrels of it!"

Slocum would have left the wagon train to their fortune had it not been for the offer of water for his horse. He had a spare canteen, but it had been too long since the mare had had more than a whiff of decent water. Two alkali waterholes had been vicious temptations.

"For my horse?" asked Slocum. He saw the man's belligerence had changed to something akin to hopelessness. Slocum had seen more spirit in the eyes of a cow about to be slaughtered for its meat.

"Sure, yeah, why not?" The grudging offer convinced Slocum he ought to take what he could and be on his way. More than that, he wanted to hear about the Valley of Spirits since Silas Baker seemed headed in that direction.

Slocum dismounted and led his horse toward the rear wagon. Like prairie dogs, children popped their heads up again. They stared solemnly at him but did not speak, as if they were afraid.

"Where'd you run across the Arapahos?" Slocum asked. The man pointed to a water barrel on the side of the wagon. Slocum figured this was the man's own rig. He pulled off the lid and let his horse drink noisily, watching her carefully to be sure she did not gulp too much and bloat.

"Like I said, back at the mouth of the Valley of Spirits."

"Getting anything out of you is like pulling out my own toenails," Slocum said. "How'd you rile them? Arapaho are peaceable folks usually."

"We started past the valley entrance, nothing more, I swear. They came boiling out, whooping and hollering like we did something nasty to their womenfolk." The man shrugged. Then his expression hardened. "We showed 'em. We fought real hard."

"Then they ran you out onto the desert," Slocum said. "You keep going in this heat, the Indians will win, only the sun will do it for them." Slocum sampled the water, then let his mare drink again, much to the man's uneasiness. Slocum felt no need to be conservative about the way he used the water. He had earned it. The man—and his family—were still alive thanks to some decent shooting on his part.

"We're tough," the man said.

"You're stupid," Slocum snapped. The man brought his rifle around, then saw the hardness in Slocum's eyes. He lowered his rifle. "Who's your wagon master?" Slocum asked.

"Don't have one. They're thieves, the lot of 'em. We can read a map as easy as they can." The man shuffled his feet a little, then looked up at his wife, sitting in the driver's box. Slocum had not noticed her before. She was a mousy woman and looked easily silenced. But not this time.

"Can you guide us, sir? You already saved us once. Can you get us to California?"

"Sarah, hush your mouth," the man said angrily.

For a brief moment, Slocum considered the offer. Letting these pilgrims go on their way was the same as signing their death warrants. As that thought crossed his mind, he remembered why he was out on the desert in the noonday heat. Silas Baker. *His* death warrant was the one Slocum wanted to sign—with a flourish.

"Got business of my own, ma'am," Slocum said politely. "You happen to see a man riding into this Valley of Spirits as you were hightailing it from the Arapahos?" Slocum directed the question at the woman, who seemed more civil than her husband. But the man answered.

"We didn't see anyone. And don't take her offer too serious. We can find our way. If you don't waste all our water."

Slocum considered putting a bullet through the bottom of the barrel. He held his anger in check. Some folks didn't know how to get along, and this yahoo was one of them.

"Thanks for the water. I wish you luck, because you're going to need it," Slocum said, swinging into the saddle. He touched the brim of his dusty Stetson in the woman's direction, saw others from the wagon train had slowly made their way back to see what was going on, then shook his head. He doubted he would ever see any of these people again, dead or alive.

He rode off, not looking back. His conscience bothered him for the first hundred yards; then the guilt at letting these lambs go to the slaughter diminished with distance. They had gotten themselves into this mess, and it was up to them to get themselves out. Slocum doubted they would ever see their Promised Land because of the attitude that they didn't need or want help.

Sometimes everyone needed help. On the frontier death came fast. So did assistance.

Following the tracks left by the wagons proved easy. The heat lulled Slocum, and he almost missed Baker's trail where it crossed the wagon path. He frowned as he studied the tracks. How Baker had passed by without being seen seemed incredible to Slocum. Or maybe the man from the wagon train had lied. Still, the desert held deep tracks for a spell since the wind hadn't blown too much. Might be they had passed days apart, Baker going into the Valley of Spirits long before the wagons had rumbled by, stirring up the Arapahos.

Slocum shook his head. Baker was only a couple days ahead of him, and certainly not more than a week. Rolling as slowly as they had been, their teams of oxen struggling against the desert heat, the wagons were a day's travel or more from the mountains. As he rode, a thought came to Slocum. Maybe it had been Baker's doing that roused the Indians. If this was a sacred spot for the Arapahos and he had blundered in during a ceremony, all the Arapahos might be willing to lift a white man's scalp.

In a way, Slocum hoped Baker had avoided the Indians. He wanted to end the man's life himself. No one backshot him and lived to brag on it. Slocum rode steadily, if slowly, in the blazing sun. After enough of the debilitating heat, Slocum started wondering if revenge was something he wanted from Baker.

When he spotted undeniable tracks—and definitely Baker's—Slocum perked up. The sun had dipped behind the distant mountains, and the desert turned suddenly chilly. Seeing the imprint in softer dirt showing the nicked right front horseshoe, exactly the way it had been on Baker's horse since he had fled from Virginia City, sent Slocum's heart pounding.

He was getting close to his quarry.

Looking up at the tall, needlelike spires of rock rising on either side of the faint track into the canyon reminded him of knives gutting the sky. The bloody red sunset completed the picture.

"So that's the way to the Valley of Spirits," mused Slocum. "Well, there's going to be one more ghost roaming around when I get through. Prepare to meet your maker, Silas Baker."

With that, Slocum urged his mare forward, and was swallowed up by the steep canyon walls and revived by the cool wind howling like some demented beast from the depths of the mountains.

2

Slocum wasn't superstitious, but found himself looking over his shoulder at every creak of hot rock cooling in the wind, every distant coyote howl, each and every time a shadow crossed the narrow path he followed deeper into the Valley of Spirits. He had to tell himself over and over there wasn't any such thing as a ghost. But the noises . . .

"Whoa, girl," he said, patting his mare's neck. He reined back and took a few seconds to look around, then heard a man moaning. Or was it only the wind? Slocum shivered, and it wasn't only from the increasingly chilly breeze whistling down the canyon and into his face. He dismounted and led his horse along the trail, studying the spoor in the dying light of the day.

The sun had long since vanished behind the high, ragged spears of rock to the west. Slocum worked in the twilight to be certain he stayed on Silas Baker's tracks. There didn't seem to be crossing canyons for the running man to take, but Slocum wanted to be certain he didn't accidentally let the man hide out and then slip back past him. Cornering Baker in some box canyon was fine with Slocum.

Even if Baker was likely to fight like a trapped rat.

Slocum heaved a sigh as he realized he wanted Baker to fight. He wanted to vent his wrath on the man for what he had done. Slocum's luck had been rotten until he had walked into that Virginia City dance hall and found hard-rock miners without any sense of odds. Baker had stolen well nigh five hundred dollars before backshooting him. Slocum stretched as he remembered the pain from the splinters cutting into his back.

His luck had stayed with him back then. He had fallen so that a long two-by-four had come between his back and Baker's derringer bullets. He could endure a couple of wood splinters rather than taking the lead. What he couldn't abide was the gnawing anger directed against Silas Baker.

Slocum sniffed the wind, catching a peculiar odor. He turned slowly, the wind against his face as he tried to figure out what the smell might be. Not wood smoke, not the dry vegetation caught on the stiff breeze. Slocum sniffed again, but the odor was gone.

He tugged on the reins and got the mare moving off the track and toward one towering stone wall at the edge of the canyon. Keeping after Baker in darkness was a fool's errand. Better to find some water and rest up, continuing the hunt in the morning. Slocum had not forgotten the fear on the face of the man in the wagon train either. The Arapahos had been real, and they had been furious. Whether the man had done something more than coming toward the mouth of this canyon to annoy them, Slocum could not say. From what he had seen of the man and the others with him in the wagon train, anything was possible.

"They might have tried to bust some sod here," Slocum said disparagingly. The dirt was thin and rocky, but the settlers didn't have good sense. Wandering through the summertime Nevada desert without a guide or wagon master told Slocum more than he wanted to know about their expertise and common sense.

He gave his mare her head and let the horse find a small puddle of water bubbling up from the ground near the rugged dark stone canyon wall. Slocum knelt and sampled the water. So much was contaminated with alkali. Not this. But it wasn't the sweetest water he had ever tasted, not with the thick mud mixed in with it.

He let his horse drink from the puddle while he rinsed out his bandanna. Using the cloth, Slocum let some of the water trickle through. A handful of mud remained in the bandanna while cleaner water came through to assuage Slocum's thirst.

He ate a can of beans and bit off a little hardtack from his dwindling supplies. Hunting would be a necessity soon, but Slocum had chosen speed over eating. It was more important for him to plug Baker than it was to eat well on the trail. There would be time later, after he had recovered his money—and put Silas Baker into a shallow grave.

Settling down, he pulled his blanket around his shoulders. He considered building a small fire shielded by an outcropping of rock, then decided against it. That odor he had picked up at dusk still bothered him. It was something he ought to recognize and didn't. Slocum drifted off to a troubled sleep, coming awake an hour before dawn.

He awoke, his hand flashing for his six-shooter. His finger tightened on the Colt Navy's trigger, but there was nothing to shoot. Only the wind stirred, moving around the sere vegetation along the canyon walls. Slocum swung around and looked up, at the rock face above him. This time he did fire. Outlined against the night-going-to-dawn sky was an Indian holding a rifle.

The flare from his six-gun almost blinded Slocum, but the wild shot forced the Indian back into his hidey-hole higher on the rock face.

Slocum hurriedly saddled his protesting horse and mounted, moving away from the relative security of his cold camp. His heart jumped into his throat when he saw movement above. He had fired at one Indian. Now he spotted a half dozen more.

The need to make a decision crushed down on him. If he went deeper into the canyon, the Indians would have him bottled up. Safer to retreat, but if he did that he would have to abandon his hunt for Silas Baker.

"I can hunt down that son of a bitch later," Slocum said, preferring to keep his scalp where it was. He had seen how angry the Arapahos had been as they attacked the wagon train. The sodbusters must have riled them up something fierce, and Slocum wasn't going to pay the debt the settlers had run up.

But as he turned his mare's face back along the trail, he saw dark forms moving to block his escape. Slocum reached for his Winchester, then knew he could never fight his way through the line of Arapahos. The first light of dawn turned the land into a dull gray from its deep shadow, revealing a dozen or more warriors. They had him bottled up tight in the narrow canyon.

Slocum wheeled about and trotted deeper into the canyon, riding the trail he had intended to follow anyway. But now he had to worry about the Indians overtaking him. This caused him to put his spurs to the mare's flanks more often than he had in the past. The horse put up with it until sunlight angled down. Then she simply dug in her hooves and halted.

Worrying even more, Slocum glanced over his shoulder. Either the dozen warriors he had spotted earlier had kept pace with him, or more had come out of the darkness to block his retreat. Considering how he had—too late—spotted the Arapahos camping higher up on the canyon face, Slocum thought these might be others. He had an entire army standing between him and the dubious safety of the deadly Nevada alkali desert.

"There's water here," he said, trying to convince himself more than his horse that he had no choice. He had to ride deeper into the Valley of Spirits, or deal with the Arapahos behind him.

Slocum rode.

As the day wore on, Slocum outpaced the trailing Indians. He had no illusions about sneaking back past them when the sun set. The Arapahos were too good to allow that—and there were so many of them Slocum would likely stumble through their camps. He settled down to the trail and hunted for any sign Baker had come this way.

One thing seemed in Slocum's favor. If he was bottled up in the Valley of Spirits, so was Silas Baker. He could worry about getting out when he finished his deadly business with the backshooting sneak thief.

"There," Slocum said, jumping to the ground. His heart raced. He'd found evidence that Baker had come this way. Kneeling, he brushed aside some of the rabbit brush hiding the partial hoofprint. To his surprise, more than a single hoofprint showed. A wagon had been pulled behind the horse—and it was headed out of the canyon. Slocum worked a bit more, brushing away dust and vegetation until he got a better view of the tracks.

"Old, really old. Months old," he said in disgust. On foot, he backtracked until he spotted part of a sign a few yards away from the tracks. Slocum tugged the sign free of the drifted dirt and brushed it off.

He shook his head as he read: *Lost Soul, Nevada, pop. 72.*

Slocum had never heard of Lost Soul, but then he had never heard of most of the mining boomtowns that had sprung up overnight like mushrooms throughout the territory. A hint of a silver strike might cause a town of five thousand to appear overnight. Rumors of gold would deplete the town of its fortune-seekers and cause another town with no good reason for existing to blossom and flourish, until the precious metal petered out or a newer, richer strike promised even grander riches.

Looking around, Slocum hunted for the Arapahos. Although he did not see them, he felt them behind in the canyon, blocking his retreat. But now he had a goal. Even if Lost Soul had become a ghost town, it was undoubtedly Baker's destination. Slocum mounted and rode steadily, reaching a small valley bounded by tall mountains on all sides. The best he could tell from his position at the foot of the Valley of Spirits, this was the only way out of the secluded bowl holding a tumbledown town smack in the center.

What surprised Slocum was the bustle of activity in Lost Soul. He had expected only cobwebs and memories. While the sign proclaiming a population of seventy-two might be exuberantly optimistic, enough people, including a few women, walked the streets to show Lost Soul was a surviving, if not thriving, town.

Slocum rode down into the town, wondering how they got supplies. There had not been any evidence of commerce through the Valley of Spirits. And the way the Arapahos patrolled the region, it wasn't likely many cargo freighters got through the canyon.

Hot, dry wind cut at Slocum as he rode down Lost Soul's main street—its only street. The few businesses open were what he might expect of a tiny mining town. That no one returned his greetings as he rode along, tipping his hat to the few women and howdying with the men, wasn't unexpected. The townsfolk were isolated and no doubt suspicious of strangers.

Especially if earlier they had run afoul of an owlhoot like Silas Baker.

Slocum reined back in front of the Prairie Dog Saloon, dismounted, tethered his horse, and trudged up the creaky wood steps to the front door. Two men coming out jumped back when they saw him, as if he were a ghost.

"Afternoon," Slocum said, brushing dust off his hat and clothing. The men glanced at each other, frightened out of their wits. Slocum watched them back away, then turn and run out into the heat. He shrugged it off. Walking to the bar, he leaned on it and called to the barkeep.

"How about a beer? Cold, if you got it."

The barkeep swallowed hard, got a dirty beer mug, and filled it from a tap. He shoved it down the bar in Slocum's direction. Slocum caught it easily. Warm. But he was so thirsty he did not care. The bitter fluid slid down his throat and left behind a hint of better beer and better times.

"You see a man come through in the past few days?" Slocum described Baker.

"Don't know nobody like that," the barkeep said, edging away.

"Hold on," Slocum said, tiring of the way the people of Lost Soul were treating him. He stood so that the worn ebony handle of his six-shooter poked up where he could get at it if he had to. Slocum wasn't going to shoot anyone but Baker, but he was getting mighty put out.

"What?" said the barkeep.

"I asked you a question, and you acted like I was the Devil incarnate. I don't reckon you get many travelers through Lost Soul, but you can act like you're glad to see me."

"Why?"

"Because I'm paying to drink your beer."

"It's on the house."

Slocum looked around at the empty saloon. "Business isn't that good. Why are you giving away your beer?"

"You want whiskey? Here." The barkeep slid a half-filled bottle down the bar in Slocum's direction.

With a movement faster than a striking rattler, Slocum grabbed the bottle and heaved it at the barkeep. The bottle bounced off the man's head, staggering him.

"That get your attention?" asked Slocum. He stalked down the length of the bar, jumped over, and grabbed the barkeep by the front of his shirt. He pulled him up and shoved him back against the wall. "What's got into people here?"

"Nothing, mister. Nothing. You get out of here!"

The barkeep was more frightened than he had any reason to be, even seeing the fire in Slocum's green eyes.

"You don't know Silas Baker?"

"I don't know nuthin'!"

Slocum released the man, and walked around the end of

the bar and out of the saloon. The Prairie Dog Saloon ought to have been the center of social life in a town like Lost Soul. But it was empty just before sundown. Miners should have been knocking off for the day and coming in to get a snootful of booze to kill the pain of their lives. Nothing. Nobody in sight.

Slocum stepped into the street and looked around. Like rats scurrying for their holes, the people of Lost Soul had vanished behind closed doors and drawn blinds. More curious than angry now, Slocum walked down the middle of the dusty street. Here and there, he caught sight of a wide eye peering out, only to vanish when the spy realized Slocum had spotted it.

Coming to a halt in front of the general store, Slocum squarely faced the open double doors.

"I want to talk!" he called. When he got no answer, he mounted the steps and went into the store. The clerk cowered behind the counter. Slocum reached down, grabbed the skinny boy by the scruff of his neck, and pulled him out. "I want you to answer some questions."

"Let the boy be," called a gruff voice from the rear of the store. Slocum released the young man, who tripped and fell to his knees. He looked to be about sixteen, with freckles and a thatch of dirty-blondish hair that no amount of bear grease could tame. More than that, he looked frightened out of his wits.

"I'm not here to hurt you," Slocum said to the boy.

"Thanks, mister. Thanks," the youth said.

"Get on into the back, Robbie. Sweep up like I told you." The older man came out. Slocum noted the air of command. This might be the store's owner. "What do you want?" the man asked.

"I need some supplies," Slocum said. "Some gunpowder and slugs for a .36 will do for a start."

"Can't help you," the man said. "We don't carry things like that."

"What?" This startled Slocum. "Is there a gunsmith in town who does?"

"Look, mister, you just rode into town. I'd advise you to go back the way you came 'fore it's too late."

Slocum remembered the Arapahos. It might be too late for that.

"I've got business here with a man named Silas Baker. You hear tell of him?" Slocum described Baker. The man's face shifted slightly, warning Slocum that the description had struck a responsive chord in the store owner but that Slocum wasn't going to hear what he wanted.

"You don't know what you're bitin' into here in Lost Soul," the man said. "Please, get out of town 'fore it's too late for you."

A plaintive quality came into the man's voice, a pleading that belied his tough talk.

"If this is such an inhospitable town, why don't you leave? You can't be making much money selling junk." Slocum looked around the store and saw nothing new. What hung on the walls seemed to have had rust scraped off before being offered for sale. Foodstuffs were at a minimum and, true to his earlier claim, there was no sign of firearms, ammunition, or anything that might be used as a weapon.

Even axes and saws were absent, as were dynamite and black miners' fuse. All that struck Slocum as curious for a mining town.

"Wish I could leave," the man said. Then he blanched. "I didn't mean that. I didn't!"

Slocum took a deep breath, wondering if he could beat what he needed to know out of the man. Then he simply turned and left, stepping into the twilight that had so suddenly seized Lost Soul. Only a few windows shone with kerosene lamps. Most were dark. Even the Prairie Dog Saloon showed little in the way of welcoming light. In Slocum's experience saloons were always the center of life in a town like this and went out of their way to come alive with light after dark.

Not the Prairie Dog Saloon, not Lost Soul.

Walking back into the street, Slocum made a full circle as he studied the town, wondering if he ought to seek out the town marshal. Slocum usually avoided lawmen, who had the unfortunate tendency to keep wanted posters, any number of which might have his face on them. Ever since killing a carpetbagger judge back in Calhoun County, Georgia, Slocum had been dodging the law. He hadn't crossed any lawmen recently, and didn't know if new wanted posters were circulated, but he had to play it safe.

Still, if the people of Lost Soul wouldn't even talk to him, he had to do something to find Silas Baker.

He had started for the Prairie Dog Saloon when a shadow moved on the ground beside the building. Slocum reached for his six-shooter, then relaxed when he saw the boy from the general store step out.

"Mister, come on o'er here. Please!"

Slocum went over. Meanwhile, a few men edged into the saloon and a ragged tune started on the piano. Otherwise the saloon was silent, as was the main street.

"What is it, Robbie?" he asked, remembering the boy's name.

"You gotta help me, mister. You just got to town, so you're all right. So far. Help me get out of Lost Soul!"

That struck Slocum as a strange request until he remembered how effectively the Arapahos had bottled up the mouth of the Valley of Spirits. Without any frontier skills, the boy might not be able to get away.

"Back down the canyon," Slocum said, "is that the only way out of town?"

"Yeah, the only way. The only way to get out alive."

"I'll make you a deal," Slocum said, seeing how agitated Robbie was. "Tell me what I need to know about Baker, and we'll ride out of here together."

"We will? Thanks, mister."

"Baker," Slocum insisted. "He's in town, isn't he?"

"In town? Heckfire, mister, he—"

The gunshot rang out at the same instant the boy's face went slack. Robbie sank to the ground like a sack of flour, dead before he could finish his sentence.

Slocum's hand moved like lightning. His six-gun came out, cocked and pointed back down the side of the saloon at . . . nothing. Whoever had shot the boy in the back was long gone.

3

Slocum swung around, his gun moving restlessly as it hunted for a target. No one showed up to investigate the gunshot. Knowing he was taking his life in his hands, Slocum hurried to the rear of the saloon and spun around, ready to shoot. The back of the Prairie Dog Saloon was as barren as the front. Dropping to one knee, Slocum poked around in the dry dust hunting for a clue as to who had so cold-bloodedly murdered the young man. The dust proved too dry to take a print.

Slocum holstered his six-gun and returned to Robbie's body. The boy lay staring up sightlessly at the increasingly starry night. Slocum reached down and closed the eyelids. He had no desire to watch the inexorable progression from believing those eyes still functioned to a cloudy certainty that the owner was dead, dead, dead.

Slocum climbed to the boardwalk of the saloon and hunted for any movement. Lost Soul might as well have been a ghost town for all the activity he saw. He went inside the saloon, amazed at the sight of such a crowd. Three men other than the barkeep drank, furtively hiding their shots of whiskey and knocking them back as if anyone coming in might tell them to stop. All three of the men had found seats at different corners of the room. They might as

23

well have been strangers for all the camaraderie they showed their fellow drinkers.

"A boy's been shot," Slocum called to the barkeep. The man sucked in his breath, then let it out slowly before shrugging, feigning how little he cared.

"Happens," was all the man said.

Slocum turned to the three customers. "You know Robbie? The boy who works at the general store? He's lying outside. Some owlhoot shot him in the back."

"Was it you?" ventured the most intrepid of the three.

"I was talking to him when he was gunned down."

Slocum saw all three men go pale under their weathered exteriors. One turned his back to Slocum, as if this might make him go away. Another kept staring at him out of the corner of his eye. The most intrepid man swallowed hard, finished his drink, and almost ran from the saloon.

"Get the marshal, will you?" Slocum called after him.

"That's not going to happen, mister," the barkeep said. "Just forget anything went on."

"And get out of town while the getting's good?" Slocum finished for him. The barkeep's head bobbed up and down before he went back to moving the dirt around on his shot glasses with a filthy rag.

Slocum had never seen the likes of the citizens in Lost Soul. Someone they knew had been murdered, and they dove for their burrows like the critter the saloon had been named after. Slocum didn't understand it. If they had all pointed accusing fingers at him and yelled for the law, *that* he could have understood. He was a stranger, new to town, and a murder had been committed. He was the likely killer.

These men didn't even do that.

For a fleeting moment, he wondered if all four of them had conspired to kill Robbie. He pushed it from his mind. None of them wore a six-shooter. The barkeep might have one behind the bar, but somehow Slocum doubted it.

"What should I do with the body?" he asked aloud, more to himself than any of the cowering men in the saloon.

He snorted in disgust, went out, and knelt beside the body, now starting to cool. At least none of the town dogs had come by for a quick, easy meal. Slocum got his arms around the boy's body, struggled to get him erect, and then flung over his shoulder. Heading down the street, Slocum vowed to stop at the marshal's office or the undertaker's, whichever he found first.

The Lost Soul Funeral Parlor was about smack dab in the middle of town. Even better from Slocum's point of view, a bright yellow light burned almost cheerfully in the front window. Staggering slightly under Robbie's weight, he went and tried the door. Locked. Slocum knocked twice before he heard movement from within.

The door opened to show a cadaverous man dressed in a long black broadcloth coat. Under it he wore a gray vest studded with pearls. A heavy gold watch chain dangled across.

"What do you want?" the man demanded in a querulous, grating voice that sounded like a grave opening up to reveal Hell.

"Got some business for you," Slocum said, although he thought it was apparent. He lowered the body and rested it against the wall beside the door. "It's Robbie, the kid who worked down at the general store."

The undertaker made a sour face, jerked his thumb over his shoulder, and said, "Get the corpse inside."

"You're the undertaker. You take care of him."

"Don't sass me," the undertaker said. As he moved, Slocum saw the undertaker wore a shoulder rig like some tinhorn gambler. The gaunt man carried two small pistols, one hung under each arm. "Do as you're told and get the body inside. Put it on that table."

Slocum struggled to get Robbie's body up and inside. He didn't understand the undertaker's attitude. Usually, diggers were obsequious to the point where Slocum wanted to puke. This one had a chip on his shoulder that must drive away business.

Dropping the corpse onto the table, Slocum stepped back. He realized there might not be another undertaker in a town this size. That still didn't make the mon's attitude tolerable.

"The funeral will set you back two hundred dollars," the gaunt man said, moving around and looking at the corpse. He went through Robbie's pockets and blatantly stuffed a few folded greenbacks into his pocket, as if this were his due.

"What's that?" Slocum asked, amazed at the man's outrageous theft—and even more outrageous demand for money.

"You deaf? I said it'd be two hundred dollars to bury the stiff."

"He worked at the general store. Go ask his boss for the money. Or see if he has family."

"No family," the undertaker said, his nose wrinkling. "He's like so many in this miserable excuse for a town. A drifter. Worthless piece of human debris." The undertaker fixed a cold dark stare on Slocum. "You going to give me the money or not?"

"No," Slocum said. "I didn't even know him. Some son of a bitch shot him down as I happened by. Nobody seemed interested in taking care of a dead body. That's how I happened to bring him here."

"To Uriah Parsons, Master Undertaker," the man said haughtily.

"Well, Master Undertaker," Slocum said sarcastically, "he's your customer now. Better get to it before he starts to smell up the place." Slocum glanced around and blinked. He had paid scant attention to the establishment until this moment.

It looked like some sultan's palace with its thick woven tapestries on the walls, fancy statues, and expensive artwork everywhere. The furniture had been lovingly crafted and seemed completely out of place in a nothing town like Lost

Soul. Soft light turned the room into something more sensuous than a viewing room for the dead.

It gave Slocum the creeps.

"You got a mouth on you, boy," Parsons said. "Might be I'll cut that tongue of yours out of your mouth and bury it outside town in the potter's field."

Slocum saw no reason to argue with the undertaker. Robbie had been murdered, and no one cared. The undertaker had made no comment about how the boy had died or fetching the marshal to look into the death. Slocum had seen about every kind of justice in boomtowns, ranging from vigilante committees to marshals so lax no crime was too heinous for them to bring an outlaw to justice. But he thought he knew undertakers—and Uriah Parsons was not knocked out of the usual mold.

Without giving voice to the retort he formed in his head, Slocum turned from the surly man and left.

"Get your ass back here! You can't just leave, not till I tell you!" shouted Parsons. "You got to pay! You'll pay dearly, I swear it!"

"Go to Hell," Slocum muttered under his breath. He had other business in Lost Soul, although watching a young man cut down rankled. In the street, Slocum looked around. The cold Nevada night did nothing to ease the heat he felt over the undertaker's attitude, the way no one even noticed one of their own citizens had been murdered, and the futility he felt at not finding Silas Baker.

"He's here in town. Robbie said as much. Now where would an owlhoot like that backshooting Baker hide out?" The best Slocum could tell, there was only one hotel in town, and it was falling down. Wood planks had curled up and pulled free of nails, leaving gaps Slocum could reach through. He walked to the front door and saw how it hung crookedly by a single hinge. He went inside.

Slocum was not surprised when the lobby's condition matched that of the exterior. Behind a plank dropped over two sawhorses, making the place look more like a cheap saloon than a hotel lobby, stood a clerk. Or a drunk who had moved in to impersonate a clerk.

"You got anyone by the name of Baker staying here?" Slocum asked curtly. He had passed the point of being polite. Nobody in Lost Soul responded when he said "please," so it was time to get what he wanted by any means possible, and then move on. The sooner he left Lost Soul behind, along with Baker in one of Uriah Parsons's cheap graves, the better he would feel.

"Baker?" the man asked, closing one eye and trying to focus the other on Slocum. "Name's familiar. Don't know why."

"You got a room?"

"Got a shitload of 'em," the man said.

"That's what this place looks like," Slocum said. "Give me a room for the night."

"That's fifty dollars."

"What?" Slocum stared in disbelief at the clerk.

"I said, that's a hundred dollars for the night."

Slocum reached over the plank and grabbed the man by the front of his shirt. "You're a highway robber."

"Make it a hundred fifty. A man's got to earn a living."

Slocum shoved him back, shaking his head. The whole town was crazy. It might have been the heat that cooked their brains, or whatever they mined had turned them plumb loco. Slocum had heard about men working with mercury going mad.

"I'd rather sleep in the stable with my horse," Slocum said.

"You look the type to appreciate that," the clerk said. A flash of fear crossed his face when he saw Slocum's reaction. He hurriedly added, "There's no livery in Lost Soul."

Slocum shoved the man back and stormed from the fleabag hotel, once more stopping in the middle of the street. The light still burned in the window of Uriah Parsons's Lost Soul Funeral Parlor. Whether the undertaker was working on Robbie or had just ignored him mattered less to Slocum now than it had. Being in Lost Soul numbed him. Being with such obnoxious people—and people who looked half-frightened out of their wits—wore on him.

He could not forget the way Robbie had begged him to escort him from town. That was an odd request. What was there stopping anyone from leaving, other than the Arapahos in the Valley of Spirits leading into town? The Indians could not be on guard all the time, every day of the year. The town had been supplied at one time by freight wagons. Tracks he had found along the canyon floor proved that much.

"Whiskey," Slocum decided. He needed to wet his whistle something fierce. From the look of the Prairie Dog Saloon, whoever stirred in Lost Soul was inside and whooping it up now.

Slocum pushed through the doors and stopped just inside to look around. He heaved a sigh of relief. This looked more like a town filled with miners. Two dozen men clustered in the saloon now, sitting at tables in twos and threes, sharing drinks and boisterously talking among themselves. But hubbub died when the barkeep spotted Slocum. It was like a fire spreading, a fire that brought not heat but cold. The silence wore on Slocum as everyone stared at him.

There had been some hint of companionship before they noticed him. Now there was only fear.

He decided to play on it.

"I'm still hunting Silas Baker," he said loudly. Men began pushing their chairs back, getting ready to bolt and run.

"Drinks on the house," the barkeep said, obviously worried. His eyes darted about. "Entertainment's starting in a few minutes. Nobody wants to miss that, do we?"

Slocum saw the curious moral battle being fought in each man's head. They all wanted to leave, yet the barkeep's words held them firmly in place—and it wasn't the promise of free booze preventing them from leaving. But what it might be, Slocum couldn't say.

"Give me one of those free drinks," Slocum said, going

to the bar. The barkeep poured, his hand shaking. Some
liquor spilled onto the bar. He hastily mopped it up and
started to go. Slocum grabbed his wrist and held him tight.

"What do you know about Baker?" he asked.

"Show's starting. Hush now," the barkeep said. Slocum
had seen rabbits run down by a pack of dogs that didn't
look this terrified. He released his grip, sampled the free
whiskey, and was pleased to find it went down smooth and
pooled warmly in his belly. He had expected the firewater
to be unbearably bad, save for the alcoholic content. Like
everything else he found in town, Slocum could not explain
the high quality of the whiskey.

He considered another drink, then decided he had to
move on. No one in the Prairie Dog Saloon was going to
tell him what he wanted to know. While it was possible
Silas Baker had them all cowed, he found that hard to believe. Baker wasn't more than a few days ahead of him
going through the Valley of Spirits. No one treed a town
like Lost Soul in just a day or two.

Not even John Wesley Hardin, and Silas Baker was no
John Wesley Hardin.

Slocum ran his finger around the rim of the shot glass,
transferred the single remaining drop to his lips, then started
for the door. He stopped when he heard the collective sigh
from the crowd. Glancing over his shoulder at the small
stage at the rear of the saloon, he saw the reason for the
reaction.

The woman who strutted out, dressed all in pink and
purple feathers and nothing more save for a skintight flesh-
colored leotard, was about the prettiest he had seen in Nevada. For all that, she was about the prettiest he had ever
seen. Blond, tall, statuesque, she was as out of place in Lost
Soul as a kind word.

Her beauty was the first thing Slocum noticed. The next
was how mechanical her act seemed. She started dancing
when the piano player banged out a tune beside the stage,
but there was no joy in the act. If someone had held a gun

to her head, she couldn't have looked any more uncomfortable.

Slocum was about to put it off as another instance of the brain fever that infected anyone living in Lost Soul when she really got into her act. Slocum's eyes widened. He had seen lewd dances before, but nothing like this. Some chanteuses and dancing girls wore skin-colored clothing that clung to their bodies but revealed less than first appeared. With this sensational blonde's act, there was more than first appeared as a large expanse showed through holes in the leotard. What Slocum saw was real skin, bare female skin, nakedness that most husbands never saw in their wives.

And how she danced!

Slocum banged into the bar, not even realizing he was that close to it.

"Another drink," he said to the barkeep, not even glancing in the man's direction. Slocum was mesmerized by the indecent dance, by the flashes of naked flesh, even rosy tips on bare breasts poking through the moving river of feathers around her body. He knocked back the drink, then motioned for a third. "Is the entertainment in Lost Soul always like this?" he asked.

Slocum didn't get an answer, nor did he expect one. He was too caught up staring in rapt fascination, feeling like a bird being caught in the hypnotic gaze of a snake. Slocum felt a little unclean, as if he was witnessing a lewd act he shouldn't have. But the woman's beauty and the way she danced so stiffly, revealing a snowy white breast, the flash of long leg, a thigh, held him in its grip.

She didn't try toying with the crowd like most dancer hall performers. Her actions were jerky and perfunctory, and when the music stopped abruptly, so did she. An expression of fear flashed across her face, quickly replaced by one of resignation Slocum couldn't understand until she spoke.

Then he was even more amazed and bewildered.

In a clear, high voice that might have belonged to a fine

chanteuse, the blond woman said, "Any man who wants
me, who wants to take me on stage, can do it. Two bits."

Slocum's heart almost stopped. The woman openly offered her favors for a quarter? And in public to any miner?
What amazed him even more was that no one jumped up
to accept her offer. The audience sat as if they had been
turned to stone. Slocum would have expected at least one
of them to be tossing coins onto stage and shouting obscene
remarks.

The only sound in the saloon was the thumping of his
own heart and the soft rustle of the feathers slithering restlessly around the lovely woman's trim body.

Slocum swung around, wondering what was going on.
Then he saw Uriah Parsons standing in the doorway, a ma-
licious grin on his hatchet face.

"My dear, I shall take you up on that generous offer. But
all I have is a solitary nickel. I'm sure this will be enough."
The undertaker walked forward slowly, sneering at those
who remained in the chairs. Flowing more like a snake than
jumping like a human, Parsons climbed onto the stage and
grabbed the blonde by the arm. He whispered something to
her. Then he dropped the nickel to the stage.

She burst into tears, shuddered, and ran away. Parsons
clung to her feather boa, grinning savagely as he watched
her streak off stage. Then started after her, twirling the
feathers and flaunting his forthcoming conquest.

Slocum had been frozen to the spot with shock at what
the undertaker did. No longer. The woman wanted nothing
to do with the odious man. Slocum didn't have to be a
mind reader to know that from her reaction. She was hu-
miliated, and some unseen coercion had been used to make
her perform such a salacious dance in front of the miners.

He reached down and made sure his Colt Navy rode easy
in its holster, then started for the stage.

A heavy hand landed on his shoulder, preventing him

from following Parsons and the blond dancer.

"Don't stick your nose where it don't belong," was the gravelly warning, followed by even more pressure on his shoulder.

4

"Don't meddle in what's no concern of yours." The words rang in Slocum's ears. He turned, shrugged his shoulder, and got his arm free of the man's punishing grip. Slocum found himself nose to nose with a man that matched his six-foot height and topped his weight by an easy fifty pounds. Slocum wasn't sure how much of that weight was fat and how much was muscle.

Stepping back a half pace pressed Slocum against the bar and allowed him to see the dull silver star pinned on the man's vest.

"Marshal," Slocum said.

"Heard 'bout you from Mr. Parsons. You don't want to mess around in his affairs. Nobody in this town does. Last thing in the world you want is to end up in the town *juzgado*."

"For being nothing more than an undertaker, Parsons seems to have a powerful lot of influence." Slocum glanced down and saw the marshal wasn't packing a six-gun. The only other man in Lost Soul who carried side arms seemed to be the mortician. Slocum found that more than a little strange, but didn't comment on it.

"We all respect and admire Mr. Parsons," the marshal said in a monotonous voice that echoed the blond woman's risqué performance on stage. There was no emotion. It was as if something had been snipped off inside and the rest of the human being simply walked around without any soul.

"Why is that?" asked Slocum. "What's Uriah Parsons done to gain your respect?" He remembered how the man had acted when Slocum had taken Robbie's body to his funeral parlor. There had been no remorse or sorrow or any hint of caring about one of his fellow citizens dying—worse, being murdered on the street not fifty feet from the funeral parlor's front door.

"You're a stranger here in Lost Soul. Don't go makin' waves or you'll regret it. We got strict laws here." The marshal's eyes dropped to the worn butt of Slocum's six-shooter. "Nobody wears guns in town."

"I'll take it off later," Slocum said. "You ought to post your laws where a stranger can read them."

"No need. Everyone knows them," the marshal said. "Hand over that smoke wagon." He thrust out a meaty hand, waiting for Slocum to meekly surrender his six-shooter.

"Reckon that's not going to happen, Marshal." Slocum didn't make a move toward the gun, but he didn't have to. He was fast, damned fast, and it showed in his stance. If the marshal tried to grab the gun or otherwise take it from him, there'd be a dead lawman on the sawdust-covered floor of the Prairie Dog Saloon.

The marshal licked dried lips, realizing he was edging closer to a bullet in the gut with every passing second. Again came that curious inner battle Slocum was at a loss to explain. It was almost as if the marshal welcomed the notion of being gunned down and only through some force of will did he decide not to let Slocum go ahead and kill him. Then the man stepped back, putting more distance between them before he spoke.

"When you decide to obey town law, you bring that piece of iron over to my office."

"You got a name, Marshal?"

"Marshal Webber." With that, the lawman swung around and left the saloon.

Slocum frowned, trying to figure out what was going on. Nobody in town sported a six-shooter. Mining camps were like that sometimes. Men spent their last cent for prospecting gear and supplies. A six-shooter or even a rifle was costly when the twenty dollars or so might buy them another case of beans and a pickax. But he had never been in a town where the law didn't go around armed—and the undertaker did.

He turned back to the bar and saw the barkeep had set up another shot of whiskey for him. He sipped at it, surprised all over again at the quality. Most saloons sold what they called trade whiskey, mixed with rusty horseshoes and gunpowder, with a little nitric acid thrown in to give the kick of a mule. But this might actually have been real Kentucky bourbon.

In the middle of the Nevada hills, surrounded by desert and angry Arapahos, he'd found a decent bottle of whiskey.

Slocum looked up to see the barkeep eyeing him strangely.

"You can't stay," the bartender said. "Don't know how you made it this long."

"What's that supposed to mean?"

"Lost Soul has laws, strict ones. You violated danged near every one of them."

"How strict?" asked Slocum, the booze going to his head a little.

"We have our share of hangings. 'Bout the only fun in this godforsaken town."

"I wouldn't say that. The blonde just provided some of the best dancing I ever saw."

"We don't talk about that, mister." If the barkeep had been warming to him, he turned distant again at mention of the naked woman with the feather boa. Slocum reckoned it had something to do with Uriah Parsons, but just what he couldn't rightly say. Even being the only armed man in town didn't give Parsons the kind of control he seemed to enjoy. A brick thrown at the back of the undertaker's head would change the odds real quick, guns or not.

"What's her name?"

"Marshal Webber probably told you to clear out of Lost Soul 'fore he found some reason to hold a new necktie party. If he didn't, let me give you some friendly advice," the barkeep said, leaning forward, hands on the bar. "Get the hell out of town."

"Doesn't sound too friendly," Slocum observed, "but it's advice I'm going to take. I need some supplies. Don't reckon the general store's open, so come first light, I'll—"

"Jethro!" bellowed the barkeep. "Go tell Mr. Caswell to open up his store. He's got a customer in a real hurry."

One of the men at a nearby table took off like a scalded dog. The hush that had fallen over the saloon grew even denser until Slocum felt it like a heavy weight on his shoulders.

"Time to buy some supplies," he said, finishing his whiskey. He trailed Jethro out the door and saw the man talking to the general store owner. By the time Slocum got to the store's door, Caswell had on an apron and motioned him inside.

"What you needin' for the trail?" the owner of the store asked.

"Answers would do me," Slocum said, wandering around, picking through the sparse merchandise. He noticed something else peculiar. For a mining town and a store supplying prospectors, Caswell didn't have any useful equipment. No fuse, no dynamite, no caps. The condition of the pickaxes and shovels Slocum had already noted. On closer examination he saw patches of rust that would make them well nigh useless for serious digging.

"Answers aren't for sale," Caswell said gruffly.

"What about Robbie?" Slocum asked.

"What about him?" Caswell crossed his arms and rocked

back, looking as if he wanted to push the whole matter away by denying anything had happened. Slocum decided it was time to rub the store owner's nose in the disagreeableness of the boy's murder.

"Somebody gunned down your clerk and you're not the least bit interested in finding out who did it?"

"Wasn't just my clerk," Caswell said, his face white with strain. In a voice almost too low for Slocum to hear, Caswell said, "He was my boy."

Slocum was past understanding. Parsons had said the boy had no relatives. Why would Caswell lie? Slocum stared hard at him and decided he hadn't. Robbie *had* been his son.

Slocum silently paid for the supplies he had taken and left. As he closed the door behind him, he heard Caswell begin to cry softly. Slocum shook his head. This was the damnedest town he had ever seen. It was time to move on and track down Silas Baker.

Slinging his supplies in a burlap bag over the rump of his horse, Slocum secured the bag to his saddlebags and then mounted. The mare whinnied in protest at the load again, but dutifully set off down the road, heading deeper into the bowl holding Lost Soul.

The stars above shone down with a coldness Slocum had seldom noticed. He felt alone on the road more than he usually did, and it bothered him now. A partner could help make sense of the puzzle that was Lost Soul. Slocum shook off the feeling of dread at the solitude as he rode along, hunting for a place to unroll his blanket and get a few winks before continuing at dawn on Baker's trail.

If he even followed the backshooting son of a bitch's trail.

A few abandoned adobe houses loomed on one side of the road. Slocum eyed them suspiciously. A good place for an ambush. When a shadow moved, his right hand grabbed for his Colt Navy. He had it almost all the way out of the cross-draw holster when he recognized the blond woman from the Prairie Dog Saloon.

"Mister, please, it's me. Yvette. From the dance hall. I saw the way you were looking at me."

"You're quite an eyeful, ma'am," Slocum said. He slipped from the saddle and walked to the woman. She held a thin blanket around her shoulders, but still shivered against the cold night breeze. Or was it only the temperature that made her shiver so?

"I . . . I have my clothes on again." Yvette shivered again. Slocum wanted to put his arm around her to share some warmth, but held back. He had the feeling of playing with dynamite.

"Is there anything I can do for you?" Slocum asked. The blonde was taller than he had thought, maybe five feet ten or so. She was even prettier up close than she had been while she danced, no matter that she was fully—chastely—dressed now. The pale starlight turned her into something almost angelic, contrasting desperately with the image of her lewd dance only an hour earlier.

"Yes," she hissed. Yvette moved closer. The blanket fell from her shoulders. She grabbed him by the upper arms and held tight, as if he might turn tall and run. "There's something you *can* do. Help me get out of this horrid place! Please, mister."

"Slocum, John Slocum," he said. He pried loose her fingers from his arms. Her grip was so hard it bruised him. "I don't see why you need my help. Just leave. Those Arapahos can't be that hard to sneak past."

"Arapahos? What are you talking about? I want to get away from *Lost Soul*!"

Slocum said nothing, remembering how Robbie had begged for the same favor and what had happened to him. He looked around, but as far as he could tell, he and Yvette were alone.

"You can do it," she said. "You're good with that six-gun. I can tell. Please, please, help me. I . . . I'll do things for you. I will!" She threw her arms around him and kissed him hard on the lips. Slocum ought to have responded, but nothing seemed right about her or the others in Lost Soul. Gently, he pushed her away.

"I don't think there's anything I can do for you," he said. "I've got other business to tend to before helping anyone else."

Yvette's shoulders slumped. "The other fellow said the same thing when he blew into town." She wiped at her dripping nose. "I need to get away before it's too late. You *got* to help me, John." Her voice rose in pitch as hysteria stole away her emotions.

"What other fellow?" Slocum asked, suddenly interested in her plight.

"The one in jail. Baker, he called himself."

"Silas Baker?" Slocum grabbed Yvette and held her as she had held him, his fingers cutting like steel bands into her thin upper arms. "Is that who you mean?"

"That's him, but he got arrested. He crossed Marshal Webber and—"

"Tell me about him."

"He couldn't help me either. Maybe he wouldn't. I don't know, since he got tossed in the calaboose real fast. I worried you'd end up there too, and then you'd never be able to get me out of town."

Slocum thought hard. Baker was locked up in Marshal Webber's jail, and he had not realized it. He might shoot the man through a barred cell window. That would be like dynamiting fish in a barrel and didn't appeal much to him. Slocum wanted to face Baker when he cut him down.

"What was he arrested for?" asked Slocum.

"I don't know, but he's supposed to swing for it in a few days."

Slocum went cold inside. He wanted Silas Baker brought to justice, but *he* wanted to be the one responsible. Stretching the owlhoot's neck was not the same as squeezing the trigger and seeing Baker die for his backshooting ways.

"I need to talk to him," Slocum said, wanting to be certain Silas Baker was locked up in the Lost Soul jail.

"I'll take you to him. Just promise to get me out of here!" Her hysterical words cut through him like a knife. Slocum realized Yvette would promise anything, promise to do anything, to escape the hell of Lost Soul, Nevada. That struck him as curious, but he had other business to deal with at the moment.

Silas Baker.

"You and your partner, you'll take me with you when you leave?" she begged.

Slocum laughed harshly, but did not correct the lovely, frantic blonde about the way it was between him and Baker.

"You stay out here. Let me talk to Baker, then we'll leave this town."

"I wish I could blow it up," Yvette grated out. With wide blue eyes turned to him, she asked, "You're not going to leave me here, are you? I told you what you wanted. You're not going to—"

"I'm a man of my word," Slocum said. If a man lost his honor, he lost everything. That was part of the reason he had to track down Baker and see that he got what was coming to him. He needed to decide if having the man's neck stretched was enough.

"Thank you, thank you," she said, kissing him hard. Slocum pushed her back, remembering what her sleek body had looked like under the feathers during her dance.

"I'll be back for you," Slocum said. He swung into the saddle and turned back toward Lost Soul and the jail. He wondered if Baker had broken the law about carrying a six-shooter in town. That struck him as funny.

He stopped laughing as he got to the end of the main street. Slocum headed to the right, going behind the single row of buildings, most of them deserted. Slocum counted buildings, went past the undertaker's parlor, and then came to a small stone hut with a curl of smoke coming out the chimney. Iron bars over a small window told him he had found Marshal Webber's domain. He dismounted and went to the window to see if he had found Silas Baker.

Peering into the small iron-strap-lined cage brought another smile to his lips.

"Hello, Baker," Slocum said. "I see you finally landed where you belong."

The man lying on the straw-filled pallet leaped to his feet and came over, grabbing the bars and pulling his face close to Slocum's.

"As I live and breathe, you found me," Baker said.

"You won't be living or breathing long, you backshooting son of a bitch," snapped Slocum.

"Aw, Slocum, I thought you were going to let bygones be bygones."

"You'll be gone soon enough. What'd you do to get a death sentence? Shoot the mayor in the back?"

Baker smiled crookedly and shook his head. "Don't take that much lawbreaking in this town, Slocum, not at all." Baker glanced over his shoulder, making certain he spoke to Slocum in confidence without the marshal overhearing. He turned back. "You get me out of this box and I'll get you out of town. I know how."

Slocum was incredulous. He had expected Baker to beg, to plead, to make false claims of being repentant for what he had done. Even claiming he'd been too drunk to remember the shooting and theft would have been in character for the man. But he was offering a trade.

Slocum got him out, he got Slocum out. It didn't make any sense.

"You've gone crazy," Slocum said. "As if you weren't loco before."

"Coming to this hellhole *was* loco," Baker admitted, "but I learned things. You'll never get away without what I know—and I don't tell you until we're a mile outside Lost Soul."

"You got sand, I'll give you that much, Baker," said Slocum. "I tracked you down to shoot you. I think I'll let the law hang you and consider justice done."

"You do that and you'll end up on the gallows too, Slocum. You don't know these people or you'd jump at my offer. Break me out tonight or you'll be sorry!"

"Burn in Hell, Baker. I'll come back for your execution." Slocum mounted and rode back toward the edge of town where he had left Yvette. Baker's mocking laughter followed him.

5

The way Silas Baker had laughed so tauntingly worried Slocum. The man was in jail with a death sentence hanging over him, yet he thought Slocum was the one who had big trouble. It might have been a ploy, but somehow Slocum did not think it was. Baker knew something and wasn't going to share it unless Slocum freed him.

"Fat chance that'll happen," Slocum said to himself. "Let him swing. I'll dance on his grave."

As he said that, he thought of Uriah Parsons and the way the man seemed to own Lost Soul lock, stock, and barrel. The marshal deferred to the undertaker in a way Slocum had never seen before, even in towns where the banker or mayor ran things with an iron hand. What puzzled him most was the lack of a six-shooter hanging at Marshal Webber's side. Towns with a tyrant as a mayor usually required the law on their side to back up their commands.

Parsons went armed; the marshal did not.

Slocum snorted in disgust. There was nothing he could figure out without spending more time in Lost Soul, Nevada—and he wasn't going to do that. He needed to talk with Yvette some more; then he would make his decision.

The mud houses began to glow a peculiarly bright silver in the moonlight as he rode closer. A flash of gold came amid the silver and Slocum saw Yvette come running out.

"You came back! I fretted about you abandoning me."
She hugged him tightly when he dismounted, like a drowning man clinging to anything that might keep him afloat.

"I promised," Slocum said, irritated with the lovely
woman for her lack of faith in him. Still, she did not know
him. Nor did he know her.

"You talked to your partner?"

"How likely is Marshal Webber to let Baker escape that
jail?" he asked.

"Nobody's ever got away, not that I heard of," Yvette
said. Her blue eyes turned to silver in the moonlight, a
strange and beautiful contrast with her golden locks. Her
hair needed washing, but it still cascaded down in honeyed
waves to dangle over her shoulders. "You're not going to
free him, are you? The marshal'd catch you for sure and
then you'd never help me get away."

"No one's ever escaped," Slocum mused. A slow smile
came to his lips. "Any chance of Baker's sentence being
overturned by a circuit judge?"

"Judge? What judge? We haven't seen a judge in more
than a year, not since Parsons came to town. Your friend's
in the lockup and he's going to stay there—until he's
hanged."

That satisfied Slocum. He heard the ring of truth in
Yvette's voice, that and a plaintive quality as her uneasiness
grew that Slocum would try to free Baker before escorting
her from this dusty valley.

"Get your belongings. We're going to hit the trail right
away."

"We are!" Yvette kissed him hard again, paused as if to
offer him more, then said, "I can go now. I don't want to
take any chances."

"You don't have anything more than you're wearing?"
This surprised Slocum. Women as lovely as Yvette tended
to have trunks filled with gewgaws and doodads and

enough clothing to weigh down the strongest of mule teams.

"I've got a blanket. What more do I need, other than you?" She hugged him again. Hot tears dampened his shirt as she clung to him and silently cried.

"You have a horse?"

"No, but I can keep up. No matter how fast you ride, I can keep up. I promise!"

"No need," Slocum said, getting onto his mare. He reached down, took Yvette's hand, and pulled her up behind him. "We won't make very good time, but we don't have to. You know any way out of here, other than back through the canyon?"

"That's the only way. This is a very large box canyon, except it's mighty wide for a canyon and they call it the Valley of Spirits. I don't know what you'd call it other than a death trap."

"How'd you come to be here?" he asked.

She put her arms around his waist and rested her cheeks against his shoulder. Again, he felt tears staining his shirt.

"I was very foolish. I came here with a fella because we were going to get rich. I cooked and washed and could sew. The silver mines meant men had need for food and clean, new clothing and we were going to give it to them."

"So what happened?"

"Jacob . . . died," she said, a catch in her voice. "Then I made a bad mistake. I had him buried."

Slocum turned to look over his shoulder at her, to see if Yvette was joking. She was deadly serious.

"I don't understand. If you don't bury a dead man, you leave him for coyotes and buzzards. That's no fit way to leave the world."

"What Uriah Parsons does is no fit way to *live* in the world," she said. Yvette fell silent, and Slocum knew she wasn't going to volunteer any more of her story. He rode along, eyes scanning the moonlit terrain ahead. The country looked different only because of the curiously dancing shadows cast by the bright moon. Otherwise, it was the same dead, desolate land he had ridden through getting to Lost Soul. He wasn't sure this might not be a better time to travel. The night was downright cold and the soul-deadening sameness of the land took on a softer aspect. And of course, he had an alluring young blond woman clinging to him, needing his strength and abilities. That would make even the dreary ride back from the Valley of Spirits enjoyable.

Seeing the dark mouth of the winding valley leading to the hot Nevada desert caused Slocum to rein back and stare into it. Blackness swallowed all detail, but he knew this route took him back to Virginia City or anywhere else he wanted to ride.

Something stirred his sense of caution. The Arapahos had bottled him up, but he had not made any real attempt to get past them. He had been intent on finding Silas Baker and bringing the backshooting bandit to justice.

"What's wrong?" she asked.

"I ran into a band of Arapaho on the way to Lost Soul," he told her. "There's something wrong ahead. Danger. But I don't think it's that war party."

Yvette shuddered and gripped him so hard her fingernails dug into his flesh. "They're blocking the way. We won't ever get away. He won't let us."

"He? You mean Parsons?"

"You don't know him. He's evil. I've never heard of a man so cruel or possessive. I certainly never met one like him."

"Parsons might carry those two pistols in his fancy gambler's shoulder rig, but he can't box us in. He's only one man."

Her short, staccato laugh irritated him. Yvette didn't come out and say it, but she thought he had already failed to get them away from Lost Soul—and Uriah Parsons.

He urged his tired mare forward, more alert than ever for trouble. He saw the hint of movement long seconds before the ambusher brought up his rifle to fire at them.

"Hang on!" Slocum cried, putting his heels to his mare's flanks. The valiant horse galloped forward, heading for a rocky patch where Slocum knew they could make a stand until he found how many men he faced. The horse dug in her hooves and kicked up a cloud of dust and gravel as Slocum got Yvette off the horse and quickly joined her. Grabbing his Winchester from the saddle scabbard, he levered in a round and waited.

The rifleman fired, betraying his position. The foot-long tongue of orange and yellow flame marked him as clearly as if he had silhouetted himself against the noonday sky. Slocum aimed and fired several times, finally rewarded with a grunt of pain, telling him he had winged their attacker.

"There're more," Yvette said, despondent. She sagged down, her long arms wrapped around herself. She brought up her knees as if returning to a fetal position.

"You use a rifle?" Slocum asked.

"No."

Slocum cursed his bad luck. If Yvette had been even a moderately good shot, he could have rushed the wounded man's position and taken him out under her covering fire.

"Be right back," he said. Slocum ignored her plea for him to stay. Ducking low, he made his way through the tumble of rock and circled, coming up on the bushwhacker's position from the side. He found the man crouched down, pressing his hand into his wounded right side. The man looked up, saw Slocum, and made the last mistake he would ever make. He went for his six-shooter.

Slocum shot him where he crouched.

Then Slocum waited, listening hard. He heard two or three more men moving around in the rocks on the far side of the trail. Figuring they were a mite leery of finding out what had happened to their partner, Slocum went hunting until he found the dead man's horse. He led it back to where Yvette cried softly.

She wiped tears away when she saw him return with the horse.

"You ride. We can get past them," he said.

"Oh, John, that's wonderful!"

"You know them? Are they Parsons' men?"

"Not exactly," she said. "It's complicated, but they'll kill us if they get the chance. They know what will happen to them if they fail." She swallowed hard and shivered, as if picturing the worst tortures this side of Hell.

Slocum was less interested in her nightmares than he was in getting by the guards at the mouth of the Valley of Spirits. He and Yvette had a few minutes when the other gunmen would hesitate to investigate what had happened to their partner. But eventually they would.

Walking their horses back past the dead body, Slocum and Yvette went another hundred yards into the canyon before picking up the pace. Twenty minutes later, Slocum heaved a sigh of relief. They had left Parsons's guards far behind. All that lay between them and the torturing heat of the Nevada desert was a rocky canyon.

"John, John!" Yvette called urgently. She rode closer and tugged at his sleeve, directing his attention to the canyon rim. For a moment he thought he was seeing a ghost, then realized the Arapaho had not abandoned their watchful lookout.

"Indians," he said. "Ride faster. They might not stop us, but you can bet your bottom dollar that they've spotted us."

Slocum quickly found he was right about one thing: The Arapahos had discovered them. The part about the Indians letting them past proved him to be wrong. Almost dead wrong.

The arrow whistling through the air took off Slocum's Stetson and spun him around in the saddle so he tumbled to the ground.

"John, are you hurt?"

"Get down," Slocum warned. "The Arapahos are ahead—

and on both sides of the trail. We aren't going to get through them now that they've seen us."

"We can't give up. I . . . I'll try to make a run for it!"

"No, don't, Yvette," he said, grabbing her by the arm and dragging her out of the saddle. His body ached from the fall he'd taken, but he hung on to her so she wouldn't commit suicide. "We need a plan."

"We need a miracle," she countered.

Slocum pushed the arrow out of his hat, ran a finger through one hole, then put the Stetson back on. Sometimes the shit fell from the sky like rain, and he wanted some small protection.

"I'll scout. You wait here with the horses." He did not wait for her to protest. He slipped away like a puff of gentle spring wind, moving soundlessly around towering rocks and past at least two Arapaho sentries. When he came to a third rank of Indians, he knew he and Yvette had no chance at all of escaping. He had thought the Arapahos would go back to their business and let the Valley of Spirits go unguarded.

He knew now he was as wrong as he had ever been in his life. Whatever held the Indians here preventing him from escaping, it was stronger than glue.

Reluctantly returning to Yvette, he settled beside the woman and brushed the dust off himself.

"Well, how do we get out?" she asked. She read the answer in his expression. The blonde sank beside him, her head back and face lifted to the moonlit sky. Tears ran down her cheeks like drops of silver. "I might have known I'd never be free."

"There doesn't seem to be any way past the Arapahos," Slocum admitted. "I might make it, but together there's no way. Even then, I'm not so sure. Never seen Indians this determined. If we did sneak past, we'd be on foot. I've been across the desert on the other side of the mountains, and there's no way we could survive out there. It's better to return to Lost Soul."

"All right, John. You tried. We tried," Yvette said, wiping her nose and putting on a brave face. She turned to him and smiled weakly. "You could have made it on your own, couldn't you?"

"Maybe," he said. "Maybe not."

"You could have, but you stayed because I'd never make it with you." She peered down at him, her eyes glowing. She kissed him, lightly at first, and then with growing passion. He tried to push her away but she was determined— and he found himself responding to her overtures.

"The Arapahos are mighty close," Slocum said. "They could sneak up on us if—"

"Yes, they could," Yvette said in a husky voice. There was lust in her eyes, but Slocum saw something else. Resignation. Life had stopped having meaning. They had not escaped the Valley of Spirits and Yvette was willing to give up.

The blonde straddled his legs and rocked back, her weight pinning his legs to the ground. She slowly unbuttoned the top button on her dirty blouse, letting the moon catch her bare white skin. Another button, more delectable flesh. By the time she finished unfastening her blouse all the way to the navel, her snowy white breasts were fully exposed. Slocum saw the cold night air—or Yvette's desire—caused the nipples to turn to hard, bronze pennies.

He reached out and cupped them. Pressing his thumbs into those fleshy pebbles told him she was excited. He felt her racing heart and knew they were fools for doing this with the Arapahos so near. And it didn't matter. He was infected with her resignation to fate, and with the need to lose himself in her.

Slocum bent over, his mouth brushing across her left breast. His tongue lightly touched the hard nubbin capping the creamy mound before he sucked the entire tip into his mouth. Yvette groaned with pleasure. He wanted to caution her to be quiet, then knew it did not matter. If the Indians found them, they found them. This was crazy, and he abandoned himself to the feelings mounting within his loins.

He moved to the other jiggling mountain of flesh, licking and tonguing as he went. His hands circled the woman's trim waist, then moved lower. He lifted her tattered skirts and found twin handfuls of sleek, naked buttocks. Yvette had not bothered with any of the frilly undergarments most women wore.

"Let me get you out where we can do something more fun," she said, reaching down to his waist. She unfastened his gunbelt and discarded it, then worked on the brass buttons holding his jeans together. With a snap, the waist button popped free. Her long, nimble fingers worked down the row of buttons holding his fly shut; then she burrowed down into the opened hollow of his pants to find the already rigid length of his manhood. The amorous blonde drew it forth.

Slocum shivered as a gust of cool wind brushed across its heated tip. Then he gasped as she lifted her hips, scooted forward a few inches, and lowered herself slowly. He pressed against the moist warmth of her nether lips. Yvette hung suspended, the thick arrowhead of his shaft barely parting her. Then she lowered herself gradually, inch by inch, taking him full-length into her moist interior. Yvette shifted from side to side, causing her breasts to sway seductively. She sighed in contentment when he reached up and cupped them in his strong hands.

"I can die happy now," she murmured as she kissed his mouth, his cheek, nibbled his earlobe.

Slocum was pinned to the ground by the woman's weight, but there was nowhere he wanted to go. He was completely surrounded by her clinging female sheath. Gripping harder on her rump, he lifted her up so that he slid slickly from her interior. When he was barely inside her, he released his grip. Yvette took her cue and dropped. Fast. Hard. Her hips ground down into his, stirring his steely shaft around in her most intimate recess.

Slocum felt as if he were a steam boiler about to blow

its rivets. Pressure mounted deep inside his body and the boiling seed in his balls threatened to come rushing forth at any instant. He fought the growing sensations, wanting this to last all night. It was a crazy place to make love, out here in the night surrounded by Arapahos wanting to lift his scalp, but he wasn't going to move. He was going to enjoy everything Yvette offered.

Gripping her breasts, he guided her up and down as he fondled those marvelous melons. The blonde threw back her head. For a heart-stopping instant, Slocum thought she was going to howl at the moon like some lovelorn coyote. But she only gasped and sobbed and moaned—and lifted and dropped around him faster. Every time she came to rest at the bottom of the stroke, her hips rotated and her back undulated, giving a back-and-forth motion that drove him wild. Every inch of her tender interior passage touched him and stimulated him even more.

Then she started grasping at him with her strong inner muscles. He felt as if he were being milked. But it was exciting, and he tried to give to her as much pleasure as he received.

Yvette rose and fell, and Slocum applied hands and mouth to the most sensitive parts of her anatomy he could reach. They were quickly past speaking. Panting harshly, they struggled together, slowly going up to the peak, where their desires exploded like falling stars.

Slocum moaned, but Yvette let out a single long, low gasp as her entire body shuddered with sexual release. They continued movement for a few seconds longer, then simply clung to one another. Yvette put her head on his shoulder and Slocum stared past her into the night, trying not to imagine moving shadows and deadly Arapaho warriors.

He wasn't sure what he had gotten himself into, but at the moment he didn't mind too much.

6

They rode back to town in silence, bathed in the cold light of the setting moon and cloaked by an increasingly bitter wind. Slocum felt the desolation more than ever, and began to understand Yvette's frustration. Trapped. That was the way he felt, but not completely. He could have escaped the Valley of Spirits, but not with the woman; for whatever reason, the Arapahos were too intent on keeping everyone bottled up in the valley for the woman to ever hope to sneak past them. Slocum shook his head. Even he would have had trouble, once past the sentries, because he needed to do it on foot. A horse would have to be stolen to cross the burning-hot desert beyond the far mouth of the canyon.

Slocum almost wished he had taken the offer to act as scout for the wagon train. It would have been dreary, boring work. Boring seemed good at the moment.

Returning to Lost Soul weighed down on him because of their failure to get free, but Slocum knew some small triumph. He could stay in the cheerless town long enough to see Silas Baker swing. Yvette had nothing to look forward to at all that he could see.

He glanced sideways at the blonde, and saw the slumped shoulders and the look of defeat that etched her features into a permanent devastation. Slocum had no idea what went on between her and Uriah Parsons, but he could guess from the way the undertaker had jumped onto the stage after her lewd dance. Slocum started to ask about that risqué performance, then bit back the question. They had shared much tonight, but he did not feel as if he knew her well enough to poke around in the most intimate details of her life. For all he knew, she had relished her paid-for-with-a-nickel liaison with Parsons, even if it had not appeared that way when she was on stage. Slocum was wise enough in the ways of the world to know things were not always how they appeared.

"We'll stay around for a spell, then leave," he told her.

She shook her head sadly. "No, John, it won't work that way. This was my one chance to get away and I failed. I'll never get another chance like this one."

"We didn't do too bad tonight," Slocum said, remembering how they had spent a delightful hour or so out in the rocks, not a hundred yards from the prowling Arapaho sentries. It had been foolish, dangerous, the riskiest thing he had done since the war had required him to penetrate behind enemy lines. For all that, it had been even more thrilling. Yvette was a skilled lover and had thrown herself passionately into the lovemaking.

"Some parts were fine," she said, smiling weakly. "I didn't get out of Lost Soul and that makes me . . . a lost soul."

"Don't cry," Slocum said, seeing the tears welling like liquid silver in her eyes. "I won't let anything happen to you."

"Is that a promise?" Her tone carried no hope now. "Don't promise me that, John. There's no way you can keep it."

"Why not?"

Yvette did not answer, turning to face straight down the dusty road leading into Lost Soul.

"Why not?" pressed Slocum. "You saying I'm not up to the chore?"

"You don't know what you're getting into," was all she said. From there on into Lost Soul she said nothing more. Slocum did not disturb her silence, content to lose himself in his own thoughts. They arrived in the town less than an hour before sunrise. For the first time he realized how bone-tired he was.

"Get out, John, get out of here while you can," Yvette said, dismounting and going toward a ramshackle house. Slocum wondered if this was where she lived—or where she plied her trade as a soiled dove.

"When I go, you'll be with me," he said.

A shadow of a smile flickered across her lips; then she turned and went inside, leaving Slocum to his own devices. He dismounted and led his faithful mare to a deserted livery. Slocum put the horse in a stall, brushed her down, and saw to a large helping of hay. He hunted around for grain but found none.

Seeing the mare wolfing down her breakfast gave Slocum the idea he ought to put some vittles under his own belt. He needed sleep, but he needed food more. Out in the street he looked around. The Prairie Dog Saloon had closed, but he was not in the market for a beer or even whiskey at the moment.

The dawn broke at the end of the main street, rays of light slipping past distant clouds to highlight a single sign a hundred yards away. Slocum started walking. He didn't much care if it was divine intervention or pure luck; the light gleamed off the front of the Lonesome Cow Café.

Slocum went in and sat down, oblivious to the dust rising and then settling around him. John Slocum and trail dust were old friends.

A waiter came over, stared at Slocum as if he had three heads, and finally asked, "You want something?"

"Breakfast," Slocum said. "I've got the money to pay for it."

The man bit his lower lip and nodded, turning to go.

"Wait! I haven't told you what I want."

The waiter looked at Slocum with his curious gaze and laughed harshly. "We don't have more 'n a pork chop with some fried taters. Take it or leave it."

"I'll take it," Slocum said, preferring a good thick slab of beef but willing to accept anything.

"You made a bad mistake, mister," said a cracked voice. Slocum saw a man even more disreputable than he was standing in the doorway. "Old Claude here don't fix nuthin' too good."

"So why do you keep comin' back, Henry?" demanded the waiter.

"You're the only place in town with any food left."

"Come on over and join me," Slocum said, gesturing to Henry.

"Thank you kindly. You're new to Lost Soul, ain't ya?"

"I am. Got in yesterday," Slocum said. "What's your game? You been here a spell?"

"Miner. Silver mine outside of town. Been here all my life, or so it seems." Henry hawked up a gob dark with blood and spat on the floor. "Reckon I'll be till I die too."

"Lost Soul doesn't look as if anyone's ever been born in it," Slocum said.

Henry chuckled, then stared at Slocum. "Nobody is *born* here, but a passel of folks *die* here. That's all there is to do. That and mine silver."

"For a silver town, Lost Soul doesn't seem overly prosperous," Slocum said, shifting in his chair for the waiter to drop an anemic pork chop and half-cooked potatoes on the table in front of him.

"Dyin' by inches, we are." Henry gobbled down his food as if it had been a month of Sundays since he had eaten.

Slocum studied the man. His appetite was not feigned to judge by the gaunt look, the sunken eyes, and the dirty, brittle hair. This was a man who had not had a square meal in a powerful long time.

"Where's the silver go?" asked Slocum, finishing his own meal and finding it wanting.

Henry shrugged and buried his face in his plate, licking up the last traces of cooking grease.

Before Slocum could ask another question, the light of the rising sun pouring through the doorway blinked out. About the biggest man Slocum had seen cast a long shadow into the café. Henry glanced up and shuddered.

"You worthless, no-account slacker. What you doin' in town when you are supposed to be at the mine workin'?"

"Got hungry. That swill you dish out ain't worth pukin' up, Conrad!"

The mountain of a man crossed the room in three quick steps. His hand came back and crashed into Henry's face, sending the scrawny miner to the floor. Slocum was not even aware he acted. He half-stood, swung, and caught Conrad in the middle of his gut. A shock ran all the way up Slocum's arm to his shoulder, telling how solid the man's belly was. But enough force had been transferred to cause Conrad to bend double, the air knocked from his lungs.

Slocum stood, measured his distance, and then kicked as hard as he could. The toe of his boot caught Conrad in mid-chest, finishing the whupping he had started. Conrad crashed to the floor and lay spread-eagle.

"Come on, get up and let's finish this," Slocum said. Then he edged closer and saw Conrad wasn't moving. His chest didn't heave up and down, gasping for the air Slocum had knocked out of his lungs. And his eyes were sightlessly staring up at the ceiling.

"My God, mister, you done kilt the mine foreman," Claude gasped out from the direction of the kitchen. The waiter vanished. Slocum heard a door slam shut at the rear of the café, but was more interested in helping Henry to his feet.

"You all right, old-timer?" Slocum asked.

"Been better," Henry said, shaking his head to see if anything had been knocked loose. When he saw Conrad on the floor, he glanced at Slocum. "He looks mighty dead.

You shoot him?" Henry's eyes darted to Slocum's six-shooter, still in its holster with the leather keeper over the hammer.

"I hit him, and he went down hard," Slocum said.

"You killed Conrad with your bare hands?" This stunned Henry more than being hit. He sat heavily and stared at Slocum with his mouth gaping.

Before Slocum could respond, Marshal Webber rushed into the small restaurant. His hands fluttered around like birds taking flight; then he calmed down. He prodded Conrad with the toe of his boot, then looked at Slocum.

"He's dead. You murdered him. Claude says so."

"He hit Henry. I hit him. The difference is that Conrad stayed down," Slocum said. He had killed men before, but never with a punch and a kick. Conrad had died almost too easy for a man that size. Slocum had anticipated a hard fight.

"I got to arrest you, Slocum. There's no way around it."

"It was self-defense," protested Henry. "Even *he* can't go against that."

"I have to, Henry," Marshal Webber whined. "It's the law. You're under arrest, Slocum."

Slocum stood and squared off. He had just killed one man. He wasn't above gunning down a second, even if it was the town marshal. The lawman didn't wear a six-gun, but Slocum wasn't going to jail, not if it meant he would be put into the same cell as Silas Baker.

In Lost Soul, Slocum knew he might just end up like Baker with a noose around his neck.

"Might be you can work it out with *him*," Henry suggested to Webber, obviously working to keep Slocum out of jail. "You know what it would take."

"Slocum, you pay for Conrad's funeral and I'll drop the charges."

Slocum didn't know whether to laugh or shoot the man for being such a bald-faced liar. Then he saw Marshal Webber was serious.

"That's all? Pay for burying him and you'll drop any murder charges?"

"The funeral'll make it self-defense. Ain't that right, Marshal?" asked Henry. "Who knows? I might even get myself promoted to take Conrad's job. Always wanted to be a mine foreman."

"Maybe you can get a square meal then," Slocum suggested.

"Pay's no better, but there's got to be some reason Conrad wanted the miserable job," Henry said.

"Come on down to the undertaker's with me," Marshal Webber said to Slocum. "I want this taken care of right now." He turned and waved to a pair of men carrying ax handles to come into the café and drag out the body. The men must have been deputies, though Slocum did not see any stars pinned to their shirtfronts. They dropped their ax handles and grabbed Conrad by heels and shoulders, grunted as they lifted, then carried him from the restaurant. Slocum doubted having a corpse in the middle of the floor did much to add to the appeal of the Lonesome Cow, not that the crowds had rushed in to eat this morning.

"Move along, Slocum. This is pretty bad news." Marshal Webber worried more about talking to Uriah Parsons than he did about murder having been done in his town.

Slocum realized the marshal did not consider Lost Soul to be his town. The way Henry had talked convinced Slocum the real power lay in front of him in Parsons's undertaking parlor.

"Mr. Parsons, sir," Marshal Webber called timorously. "I got a problem I need you to deal with."

"Who died?" asked the dour undertaker. The man's eyes gleamed when he saw his guess was correct, that some poor wight in Lost Soul had died.

"Conrad, sir." Marshal Webber glanced over his shoulder. "Him and Slocum got into a fight down at the Lonesome Cow. It was self-defense. There was witnesses, and Slocum says he'll pay for the funeral." The last explanation came out in a rush, as if it made everything all right.

"I've been over a similar matter with him," Parsons said in a particularly nasty tone. "Will this time be any different, Mr. Slocum?"

Slocum considered his options. He could fight off the marshal and his ax-handle-wielding deputies, but turning the town against him didn't seem too good an idea. Things were far from normal in Lost Soul as it was. He did not need a vigilante committee coming after him, thinking his death would make their own lives any safer.

"What'll it cost to plant him all proper-like?" Slocum asked.

Parsons rubbed his hands together and looked as cheerful as Slocum had ever seen him. "I need to consult with my wife on how best to proceed." Parsons turned and bellowed, "Purity! Purity! Get on out here. We have a customer."

From the back room came an older woman, her graying hair pulled back in a severe bun. She wore heavy rubber gloves and stank of embalming fluid. In one gloved hand she carried a large knife with gore dripping from it.

"What the hell you want, Uriah?" she demanded.

"Conrad's dead. We got a chance to bury him, no worry about expense."

Slocum started to protest, then bit back his words. He was not going to rock the boat now. These were unpleasant people, and he wanted nothing more than to be done with them.

"Conrad's dead? What you going to do about that, you ugly son of a bitch?" she directed at her husband. Uriah Parsons stiffened, and might have throttled her if she had not held the knife so firmly.

"We're going to bury him, you old harridan," Parsons snapped. "You think a hundred dollars is a fair price?"

"Make it two hundred," Purity Parsons said. She turned to Slocum and looked him over from head to toe. An unpleasant smile came to her thin lips. She pushed back strands of her graying hair, leaving bloody streaks wherever she touched. "You the one who gave Conrad what for?"

"Yes, ma'am," Slocum said.

"Come on back into my office and let's talk this over," she said. "Might be we can work out something."

"What?" Slocum asked point-blank.

"Why, it might be a matter of you scratchin' my back so I can do the same for yours," she said, leering at him. Her yellowed teeth were uneven. Slocum saw one was black and about ready to break off. What disgusted him most was her unabashed lust.

"You old—" began Uriah Parsons.

"You shut that foul mouth of yours," she snapped. "Me and Slocum were discussing what he might do to cut the cost of the burial for the man he laid low."

"Don't see how you can cut corners," Slocum said. "It's not necessary to put Conrad down into the ground with a first-class ticket."

"The son of a bitch never went first-class anywhere," Purity Parsons agreed. "Now, you, you got the look of a mighty fine Southern gentleman about you. Let's go into my room and—"

"Mr. Parsons said two hundred would cover it. That takes about all my poke, but I can cover it," Slocum said, counting out the money. He was close to flat broke now, but he wanted no part of Purity Parsons or her thinly veiled lewd suggestions.

"Why, you little ingrate. I was offering you paradise and you turned it down?" Purity Parsons lifted her knife to slash at Slocum, but her husband grabbed her wrist and wrestled the bloody blade from her grip.

"The marshal heard the price, didn't you, Marshal Webber?" Slocum asked.

"Well, I might have—"

"Two hundred," Slocum said, dropping the money on a closed coffin at the side of the room. "Reckon this sends Conrad off in style. Anything more you need from me, Marshal?"

"I—"

"Good day then," Slocum said, leaving the battling husband and wife with the marshal in the funeral parlor. He stepped into the pure, clean sunlight, feeling as dirty as if he had slithered on his belly through a clogged sewer.

Whether Yvette went with him, Slocum vowed to leave Lost Soul as soon as he saw Silas Baker's neck stretched.

7

Slocum did not know what to do with himself all day long, so he sat in a chair on the boardwalk outside the Prairie Dog Saloon, watching as people passed by him and trying to figure out what made the town tick. He was as lost as the Lost Soul in the town's name. Nothing made much sense to him. For all the talk of a fabulous silver strike somewhere outside town, no one had any money. Most of the residents appeared on the verge of starving to death.

The only prosperous residents of the town were Uriah Parsons and his wife, Purity.

At the thought of the odious woman, Slocum spat. She was a grotesque creature who had obviously taken a shine to him. He wondered if many of the hollow men in town went along with her lewd suggestions, of if they moved her to make such advances to them. Looking around, he considered how likely someone starving to death was to agree to anything she might propose. She and her scurrilous husband had cornered most all the money in town by watching people die. At that thought, Slocum touched his shirt pocket where his poke had ridden until recently. Still, paying them their blood money to bury Conrad in a style he had never earned was better than being sent to jail.

He had walked past the gallows constructed at the south

end of town. Most law-abiding places considered a single platform adequate to the needs of enforcing sentences meted out by a judge, even a hanging judge like Isaac Parker back in Arkansas. This one had three trapdoors, with the knotted nooses dangling above, twisting slightly in the hot wind blowing through Lost Soul. Somehow, Slocum did not doubt the marshal put down three men at a time, and from the talk around town, it happened with some regularity to men who crossed the undertaker or his wife and to those unable to pay their debts.

This thought worried Slocum a mite more than it usually did. He had less than two dollars in coins jingling in his pocket. At the prices charged in Lost Soul, that wouldn't last long. It was time to think about moving on, especially since it seemed that damned little was for sale at any price.

"After Baker swings," he told himself. Slocum had not gotten any idea of when this might be from Marshal Webber. The lawman seemed reluctant to mention anyone dying, whether it be by rope or gunshot. It might have been superstition on the man's part, or it could have been something more. Talk about death too often and attract the undertaker's attention?

Slocum knew the townsfolk's primary pursuit. Whatever they did, they avoided being noticed by Parsons and his wife.

"What's that, Slocum?" a voice said.

Slocum looked down to the dusty street to see Henry trudging along. The miner dropped a burlap bag and sank down on it as if it were more comfortable than the chair standing empty beside Slocum.

"Just thinking on when to leave Lost Soul."

"You missed your chance. Uriah's got his eye on you now." Henry spat, and something approaching a leer came to his lips. "Hell, man, you done attracted *her* attention. That's the kiss of death in Lost Soul. You ain't never gonna leave this godforsaken place."

Slocum shrugged that off. He studied Henry and the

coarse bag under him. Seeing his interest, Henry laughed harshly, a short staccato burst more like a crow's caw than a human utterance.

"They run me out. I thought I'd take Conrad's place, but they didn't want nuthin' to do with me."

"Because you were seen with me?" Slocum guessed.

"Nobody at the mine would say, but I reckon you hit the bull's-eye with that one, Slocum. You signed my death warrant. The food at the mine wasn't fit for man nor beast, but it's better than nothing, which is what I get now."

"What have you been using your wages for?"

"Wages? Ten cents a day don't go far, especially when they charge twice that for water. It's mighty hot in that hole, believe you me. I ended up owing them danged near two dollars." To emphasize his point about the heat in the silver mine, Henry swiped at his forehead. Slocum saw blood oozing from several shallow cuts. It looked as if they had done more than simply fire the man.

"What'll happen to you?" Slocum asked.

"They might swing me alongside that fella you know— what's his name?"

"Silas Baker," Slocum said softly, remembering Baker had claimed to know a way out of Lost Soul. Slocum wondered if the man actually knew of such a route or if it had been a bluff intended to coax Slocum into breaking him out of jail. For all his backshooting ways, Baker had been a fair poker player. Not an honest one, but good enough to stay with Slocum at the table for an hour or so.

"That's him. He came off all brass and vinegar and it caught up mighty fast with him. No one sasses Uriah Parsons in this town, no one."

"Parsons owns the silver mine, doesn't he?" asked Slocum.

Henry closed one eye, tipped his head, and peered at Slocum. Then he shrugged. "What's the difference who owns it? Fact is, I don't rightly know who's collecting all the silver from that hole in the ground, 'cept I know it sure as hell ain't me."

"Why don't you leave?"

"You've tried," Henry said. "I can read a man like a book, 'cept I can't read. But I see it in your face. You tried and you're still here."

"I have my reasons."

"Yeah, like that galoot over in the calaboose. You hate him so much you want to watch him die. Or is it something else? Maybe you want to break him out of there?"

"I'd sooner empty my six-gun into his belly," Slocum said coldly. Henry nodded, spat, then hefted his bag.

"See you around, Slocum. 'Cuz you ain't gettin' out of this hellhole any more 'n I am." With that Henry started walking—to where, Slocum couldn't determine, but he doubted it was out of Lost Soul.

Lost Soul was filled with lost souls.

The sun dipped below the rim of mountains forming the Valley of Spirits and turned the air downright cold. Slocum shivered a little, then stood and glanced into the Prairie Dog Saloon. All day the slow trickle of customers had not amounted to more than five men. This ought to be the peak hours, right after the workday ended in the mines. But three men sat in the saloon, one in each corner, each suspiciously glaring at the other two. The barkeep stood idly behind the bar, looking nervously at the slowly ticking Regulator clock mounted on the wall as if he waited for the last chime that would signal the end of the world.

For all Slocum knew, he might hear it.

Stretching, Slocum walked along the creaking boards, past the general store and in the direction of the cribs where Yvette had gone after their abortive attempt to escape through the canyon. He stopped and stared at the dark rectangle marking the entrance to the woman's dwelling. From the size of the building, he doubted she lived in anything more than a six-by-eight room. If asked, Yvette might claim she was happy to find such elegant digs in Lost Soul.

He walked slowly into the darkness, and was swallowed up immediately. Slocum peered down the narrow hall, wondering which was Yvette's room. Listening carefully at each door revealed amorous activities in some, deathly silence in others. But the last door in the hallway stood ajar, letting a pale yellow slice fall out onto the dusty floor.

Slocum reached for his six-shooter when he recognized the voice coming from inside the room.

"Parsons," he said, venom dripping off that single name. Slocum edged closer, opening the door a fraction of an inch more to peer into the room. He had been right about this being Yvette's. She sat cross-legged on a thin straw pallet spread across the far end of the room. If Slocum had tried lying down, he would have bumped his head on one wall and had his feet kicking through the other. It wasn't even six feet wide where she sat, huddled in on herself as if this would protect her from Uriah Parsons.

"Do it," Parsons said in a voice that brooked no argument. "Drink it!" He thrust out a small glass filled with a blood-red liquid that sloshed over his fingers. Parsons held it, then shifted slightly, letting Slocum see the undertaker held a derringer in his other hand. He was forcing Yvette to drink whatever was in the glass.

Slocum started to gun the man down, then hesitated. He had no idea what was going on. Before he could figure it out, Yvette reached out, took the tumbler in both hands, and gagged down the blood-colored fluid. A flush came to her face, and Slocum thought she was going to choke. She handed back the glass.

Parsons knocked it from her hand, sending it crashing against the wall, where it broke. Shards filled the air with tiny dazzling reflections as they scattered and fell to the floor.

"I'll see you later," Parsons said, making it sound obscene. He swung about and headed for the door. Slocum anticipated the undertaker's departure and dashed for the front of the cribs, ducking around to the side as he waited for the man to come out. He would settle the score here and now when Uriah Parsons emerged.

The undertaker never did.

Slocum hazarded a glance back down the narrow hall and frowned. Wherever Parsons had gone, it wasn't out this way. Slocum had not seen a back door, but he must have missed it. Hurrying back down, he pushed open Yvette's door. She sat on the floor, her legs drawn up and arms holding them tightly to her body. She rested her head on the top of her knees and sobbed softly. When she looked up, it was as if she stared through Slocum rather than at him.

"What's wrong?" he asked. Slocum knelt and picked up the largest piece of the glass tumbler. He ran his fingers over the inside. It was damp, but all color had vanished now. It might have been nothing more than water in the glass for all the odor and feel. He started to taste the drop, but Yvette moved faster than he would have thought possible as she grabbed his wrist.

"John, no! Don't!"

"Why not? What was that red stuff Parsons made you drink?"

"I . . . I can't tell you," she said, shuddering as if she had contracted the ague.

"Well, enough of that then," Slocum said, not wanting to push the point. He was fed up with Parsons and his wife, and came to a quick decision. Let Silas Baker hang without him in the audience. "Get your belongings together. This time we'll sneak past the Arapahos and—"

"No," she said, her voice almost breaking with emotion. "I can't, John. Not now."

"Why not? It won't be easy, but I have an idea how we can do it. We get past the Indians, then steal a couple ponies. That'll get us across the desert and more than halfway to Virginia City."

"I can't, John. I had my chance and lost it. I have to stay here now, or—"

"Or what?" he demanded.

"Go on without me, John. Leave while you still can. And wash your hands real good."

"I don't understand what's going on, Yvette."

"It's too late for me. Now go, go, *go!*" She broke down, openly crying now. Slocum was disgusted with her and left, but he barely reached the door to the cribs when he ran smack into Marshal Webber. The lawman recoiled, then reached out and grabbed Slocum by the arm to keep him from walking on.

"Hold it, boy," the lawman said.

"What do you want?" Slocum said more harshly than he intended. He was put off by Yvette's behavior and wasn't likely to take anything from anyone in Lost Soul, including the marshal.

"You violated a trespass ordinance," Webber said, licking his lips and looking nervous.

"What?" Slocum spun around and jerked free of the man's grip. His temper flared and his hand twitched slightly. It would not take much for him to go for his six-shooter, though the marshal wasn't armed. Slocum didn't cotton to gunning down unarmed men, unless they riled him.

Marshal Webber was riling him something fierce.

The lawman read the nearness of dying in Slocum's blazing green eyes and backed off, but he didn't change his tune.

"You're trespassing on private property. Nobody asked you here. That's a fifty-dollar fine."

"What happens if I don't pay it?" Slocum asked.

"Jail," Marshal Webber said simply.

"No."

"Then I'll take that smoke wagon of yours." Webber reached out to pluck Slocum's Colt Navy from its holster. Slocum grabbed the man's wrist and twisted savagely, sending the marshal stumbling. Before the lawman could recover, Slocum had slipped off the leather thong holding the six-shooter in place. He squared off, ready to throw down on the man, armed or not.

"Nobody takes my six-shooter," Slocum said in a voice laced with the promise of death.

"You can't go around Lost Soul breakin' our laws, Slocum. We got ways of making you pay for that," the man said. He backed off, turned, and then almost ran away. Slocum knew the man could scare up his deputies and the trio would come looking for him. They might not be armed, but sooner or later he had to sleep, he had to turn his back, he had to let down his guard. When he did, an ax handle would crash into his skull, sending him to the promised land—or worse.

He might wake up in the jail next to Silas Baker.

And the thought kept intruding that Henry had said they hanged debtors in Lost Soul. Trespass might not be a hanging crime elsewhere, but it just might be in this town, if Uriah Parsons said so.

Slocum sneered at the thought of leaving his fate to either the undertaker or his wife. He had not won many friends in Lost Soul, least of all those two.

It was time for him to take the bull by the horns and make things happen rather than waiting for them to happen to him. Slocum pushed past the marshal, waiting for him to protest. Marshal Webber held his tongue and did not follow him. Instead, the lawman went into the cribs.

Slocum headed for the jail, but not to turn over his six-shooter. At the rear of the *juzgado* he peered through the small window into the cell. The thick iron straps circled the walls and ceiling. Slocum could not tell, but thought they went under the flooring too.

"That you, Slocum? Yes, it is. I thought you'd be back 'fore now," came Silas Baker's mocking voice. "I heard how you got the marshal all stirred up when you killed the mine foreman. Webber find you yet?"

"We've had words," Slocum said. "What's going on in this town?"

Baker laughed without even a hint of merriment. He shook his shaggy head and said, "You should have figured that out by now. You've seen towns where only one man held the reins."

"Parsons," said Slocum.

"He's the head sidewinder around here. Him and his wife. But you don't need me telling you that. Are you ready to break me out?" Baker twisted around, listening hard as Marshal Webber crashed around in the small adjoining office like a bull in a china shop. The lawman harangued his two deputies about Slocum and how he was a lawbreaker needing to be brought to justice.

"You got them stirred up something fierce, John," Baker said, smirking. "You better get me out of here pronto."

"Tell me what's going on. Why isn't there any food in this town? Why do the Arapahos bottle up the canyon leading into the Valley of Spirits? Is this some kind of sacred ground for them?"

All he got was Baker's mocking laugh.

"Tell me, damn you."

"Damn me? Yep, reckon that's exactly what I am, a damned soul. But I want to be a *free* damned soul. You catch my drift?"

Slocum thought a moment. It rankled to need Silas Baker for anything, much less information.

"Get me out of here, Slocum. Now, John, now!"

"I'll think on it," Slocum said, turning and walking off.

"Don't wait too long or *you'll* be the damned soul!" were Baker's parting words.

8

Slocum stirred and pulled at his blanket, only to find it was gone. He growled like a stepped-on cougar and sat up, looking around. He had spent the night in the stable in the stall next to his mare because he lacked the money for a room, even if one had been available without bugs to gnaw at his flesh. The straw wasn't fresh, but it also was cleaner than any bed he was going to find in Lost Soul. He groped for his blanket and did not find it.

"Where'd it go?" He sat up. His mare poked a large brown eye over the top of the stall and whinnied. Slocum searched for the blanket but couldn't find it. Puzzled, he rose and brushed himself off. In the middle of the stables, clearly outlined in a pile of old horse manure, was a fresh boot print. Reconstructing the intruder's path to the back door was easy enough for a greenhorn.

"I'll be damned," Slocum said, scratching his head. Someone had sneaked into the livery and had stolen his blanket while he slept. "If it's not nailed down in this town, it gets stolen. And if they do nail it down, I bet the nails'd be stolen too."

Slocum made sure the mare was well tended, then left, surprised to find the sun up already. He had slept the sleep of the dead. As that thought crossed his mind, the irony of it hit him. Lost Soul was a town where the dead ruled—or at least the undertaker. Across the street Slocum saw Uriah Parsons strutting along, people jumping out of his way as if he were some kind of European royalty.

Slocum's hand went to his six-shooter, then relaxed. If the midnight thief had tried to take his six-gun, Slocum would have noticed. As it was, he was increasingly reduced to pauper status with every day he remained in this flea-bitten town.

But too many questions remained unanswered. What was Parsons's hold over the people? What had he forced Yvette to drink? She had been well nigh impossible to talk to about it. She might as well have seen her own death coming for all her resignation after downing the blood-red fluid.

Slocum crouched down at the corner of the stable as the marshal and his two deputies made their morning rounds, rousting men sleeping under the boardwalks and in alleys. He had never been in a town where the lawmen weren't weighed down with three pounds of firepower on their hips. In the few towns where the marshals didn't bother with six-shooters, they usually carried scatterguns for crowd control. Still, the lack of six-shooters did not hamper Marshal Webber or his two men. From what Slocum had seen, this was a law-abiding town.

He glanced to the far end of town where the three gallows stood like gaunt vultures, their cross-members bent down like a buzzard's neck and the knotted ropes mocking, dangling tongues. Dead men tended to be real peaceable.

Slocum had to wonder how long it would be until he crossed the line and Marshal Webber arrested him for some trivial crime that carried the death penalty. Trespass was hardly a crime, especially when he had been in the town's whorehouse. That meant Webber had his orders to jail Slocum whenever he could. It didn't take much of a genius to know whose orders those were either.

The Colt Navy slid easily from its holster and pressed comfortingly into his palm. Slocum spun the blued cylinder, making sure each chamber carried a round. He needed to dig through his saddlebags and find a couple of extra cylinders, in case he got into a fight requiring fast reloading. It was easier to knock out the entire cylinder and replace it with one carrying six loaded chambers than it was to reload.

He shook himself and wondered at the way his thoughts wandered. Lost Soul brought out the worst of his pessimism. Or maybe he was catching some of Yvette's depression. He had seldom seen anyone so down in the mouth as the lovely woman.

"Come on, big boy. You're just what I need to while away some time."

Slocum swung around at the sound of the shrill voice he knew all too well from the single time he had met the woman. Purity Parsons had not seen him. Across the street, she sidled up to a scrawny miner and ran her hand over his stubbled face. The miner looked as if he might lose his last meal, whenever that might have been, but he did not shy away from the woman. She kept on stroking his face and shoulders and arms—and then worked lower. The miner jerked when she grabbed his crotch and squeezed down mighty hard.

"I know what they mean by hardrock miner now," she said lewdly. "Come on along."

Fascinated in the same way a bird is mesmerized by a snake's darting tongue, Slocum trailed the two as they made their way down the street to the funeral parlor. Purity led the miner inside, but did not close the door tight enough to keep the brisk furnace-hot breeze whipping along the street from snapping it wide open.

Standing outside, Slocum got a good look inside. His stomach churned when he saw the woman feverishly unfasten the miner's canvas britches and then push him backward into an open coffin. Then she leaped on him like a dog on a bone.

Slocum turned and headed back toward the Prairie Dog Saloon. He had seen men blown apart by cannonballs, tram-

pled by stampeding cattle, and even crushed beyond rec-
ognition when they were hit by a locomotive, but none of
it sickened him quite as much as what he had just seen.
The miner had been unwilling to be Purity's partner—and
he had gone along meekly, as if she had him on an invisible
string.

It made no sense to Slocum. But then, nothing in Lost
Soul made much sense. Somehow, the undertaker and his
wife were the axle around which the entire town turned
slowly, and mixed in with it was the red liquid Uriah Parsons had forced Yvette to drink at gunpoint. The expression
on the blonde's otherwise-lovely face had been bleaker than
any desert and more desolate.

He peered into the Prairie Dog Saloon, but saw nothing
to draw him. Slocum kept reminding himself of the lack of
money riding in his shirt pocket. Two dollars, hardly
enough to buy a decent meal in this town. He moseyed on
until he came to a stretch of buildings long since abandoned. Boarded-over windows hinted that the occupants
had left with plenty of time to preserve their buildings in
hope of returning some day.

The assay office was closed, as were the courthouse and
what appeared to be a bakery. Slocum hastily corrected
himself. Once, it had been a bakery. Now it was a hollow
shell, a hint of its former glory, like the citizens of Lost
Soul.

He turned back and ripped away a board from the rear
window of the assay office so he could peer inside. The
dark interior had been stripped, leaving behind only a few
counters and a broken-down chair. All the equipment was
long gone. Slocum moved on to the courthouse, a question
coming to him he wanted to answer. With nothing more
than his hands, it took several minutes to pry loose enough
boards to open a space large enough to wiggle through.

Inside the courthouse, Slocum coughed and choked on
the heavy dust. The records he sought were on the second
floor, up a precarious staircase. Walking gingerly, he made

his way to the section where maps of the surrounding countryside—maybe all of the Valley of Spirits—should have
been kept.

The light filtering through the dirty windows afforded
him enough illumination to see that two entire shelves of
records were missing. Whistling "Tenting on the Old Camp
Ground Tonight" as he searched, Slocum went through
every volume left on the shelves. Three times he whistled
the song before he finished with the realization that no map
of Lost Soul existed.

They were all gone, as were the surveyor's plats, along
with any paperwork showing ownership of real property in
the Valley of Spirits. It was as if someone had gone over
all the records with a fine-tooth comb and removed them.

"Someone?" Slocum mused aloud. He smiled without
any humor. He knew who that "someone" was likely to be.

He spent another half hour searching the rest of the two-
story courthouse, thinking the land deeds might have been
moved. He found nothing showing who owned the land,
the mineral rights, the water rights, anything at all.

Leaving the way he had come in, Slocum wandered the
main street hunting for any other place that might have a
map of the Valley of Spirits. Caswell at the general store
refused to even speak to Slocum when he went in to inquire
about maps. That hardly surprised him since the store
owner still bore him some malice over Robbie's death, or
so Slocum figured.

Back in the hot noonday sun, Slocum squinted as he
studied those businesses still open in town. One that might
have helped was a bookstore across the way, but when he
looked inside, he saw most of the books had been removed.
What remained proved no help at all—and that included
the surly clerk. Slocum got the idea he had become a skunk
at a formal dinner party.

He left, knowing his hunt for a map of the valley was at
an end. The maps had all been destroyed. Why wasn't too
hard for him to figure out. Parsons had gunmen posted at

the mouth of the canyon leading into the Valley of Spirits.
And the Arapahos beyond did a mighty fine job of con-
taining anyone wanting to leave. With that route doubly
closed, another had to be found.

Without a map of the region, that meant a lot of riding
and hunting and probably wandering down dead ends for
a week or two. The prospect didn't set well with Slocum,
but he saw no way around it. Heading for the stable to
saddle his mare, he spotted Uriah Parsons leaving his funeral parlor in what could only be described as a furtive
manner.

The undertaker looked around guiltily, then dashed
around the building toward the rear, as if he did not want
anyone to see him. Curious at this behavior from such an
arrogant man, Slocum edged his way between two stores
constructed far too close together for fire safety until he
reached the back where an alley might have been had Lost
Soul had more population needing buildings. He squeezed
through to the rear in time to see Parsons snap the reins on
a team hitched to a buckboard. From the way the buckboard
jumped and bounced, it carried a mighty big load behind
the undertaker.

And from the way Parsons whipped the team, he was in
a powerful hurry to get somewhere out of town. This was
enough to convince Slocum his hunt for another way from
the Valley of Spirits might be shortened if he simply trailed
Parsons.

Slocum walked quickly to a spot behind the funeral parlor and looked at the tracks. The depth of the buckboard
wheels confirmed what he had seen. Whatever Parsons carried was heavy, damned heavy for such a wagon. Slocum
kept walking briskly, ducked into the livery, and saddled
his mare. The horse turned sad brown eyes toward him, as
if begging to leave Lost Soul.

"Soon," he said to the horse. He led the mare outside
and mounted, walking her slowly after Parsons. Parsons
could not keep his team pulling at such speed or he would

kill them. That meant the undertaker wanted to get out of town and out of sight before slowing his pace. Slocum saw no need to rush.

He rode out of town, aware of several people looking surreptitiously at him from behind curtains and around corners. Did they envy him his departure or did they curse him? Slocum did not care. His business in Lost Soul was about over. Let Silas Baker swing and Slocum could get out of the Valley of Spirits before the sun set a second time.

Topping a rise, Slocum got a good view of a shallow depression with a dirt road cutting across it. The area lacked much in the way of grass, allowing even the feeble wind to kick up dust in places. Here and there dust devils whirled, but one particular cloud caught Slocum's attention. That one was larger and must be Parsons and his wagon.

He made his way over to the twin ruts that passed for a road through the sunbaked land, and followed until he came to a deep arroyo. Slocum frowned. There was not any way Parsons could have navigated the steep bank on either side of the arroyo. And the sandy bottom, while it would not hold a track, showed no sign of recent passage.

Slocum couldn't figure out how he had lost Parsons, unless the man had cut off the road a ways back, heading for the distant range of mountains forming the barricades around the valley. He wheeled his mare around and backtracked, looking for a spot along the road where Parsons had left. He had been lulled into thinking Parsons would head wherever the pitiful excuse of a road went. That was not the way to proceed in such dangerous circumstances.

"Here it is," Slocum said to himself when he found the cuts in the baked dirt where Parsons had driven his buckboard. He stood in the stirrups to see if he could spot the dust cloud kicked up by the undertaker, then sank down. Slocum looked around for cover, settling on another arroyo lined with mesquite trees.

"Giddyup," he said, putting his spurs to the mare's

flanks. The horse whinnied in protest, then put on a burst of speed in response to Slocum's goading. He got the horse into the dry riverbed and then dismounted, leading the mare to a spot where he could tether her to a thorn-studded mesquite limb. The horse carefully thrust her nose into the small leafy limbs and began nibbling at the bean pods.

Slocum drew his Winchester from its scabbard and made his way to the edge of the arroyo and peered over. Not twenty yards away rode five men, all armed. That sight alone reminded Slocum of the only others he had seen in the Valley of Spirits carrying guns.

The sentries guarding the mouth of the canyon leading from Lost Soul and back into the Nevada alkali desert had carried rifles. These men must be part of that elite group, though they hardly looked like select troops to him.

Even the town marshal went unarmed, but these riffraff carried rifles and also wore six-shooters. Slocum lowered his rifle and sighted on the lead rider, wondering if it would come down to a fight with the five men. If it did, he wanted to take as many out of the fight as quickly as possible to even the odds.

His finger rubbed restlessly on his trigger, then slipped off. The men had not spotted him and rode on, heading at an angle to the rutted road he and Parsons had taken from town. Wherever this posse rode, it wasn't to Lost Soul.

Armed guards patrolled the empty countryside. Others prevented anyone from leaving Lost Soul, even if most could never get past the Arapahos also in that canyon. Who else in the Valley of Spirits went armed?

"Parsons," Slocum said, turning the name into a curse. He remembered the derringer the undertaker had held on Yvette when he forced her to drink the mysterious red liquid.

Slocum hunkered down, his back to the crumbling side of the arroyo, waiting with growing impatience. He felt like an angry bull responding to a matador waving a red flag. Normally patient, Slocum found himself wanting to beat the information out of Parsons about what was going on in Lost Soul.

Ten minutes passed and Slocum stood, checking where the tight knot of men had ridden. Not even dust in the air remained to show their passage. He returned to his horse, pulled her away from the dubious meal of dried mesquite pods, and mounted. It was time to get his answers and clear out of there.

Slocum got back to the place where he had left off tracking Parsons, rode less than a half mile, and lost the track entirely when he came to a rocky patch. An hour later, after three circuits of a large expanse of the area, Slocum had to give up. He looked toward the mountains, wondering if Parsons had gone there or if he had paralleled the range and headed farther to the south. Lacking any elevation where he might get a good look at the land discouraged Slocum.

"The hell with it," Slocum said, disgusted. Using his bandanna, he mopped at the river of sweat running down his face. In spite of the easy ride, he felt how his horse had tired, mostly from the heat. Slocum realized he wasn't up to snuff either, and made his decision.

He had no desire to run afoul of the armed men. Returning to Lost Soul, waiting for Baker to hang, and then clearing out appealed to him more and more. At least he could find shade to sit in along the town boardwalk. Even his mare seemed to agree when he gave up the hunt for Uriah Parsons and headed back to Lost Soul.

9

Slocum got back to Lost Soul a little before sundown, tired, thirsty, and disgusted with himself for his lapse in attention to tracking. Letting Uriah Parsons sneak off the way he had was inexcusable. Slocum knew he ought to have tracked a buckboard to Hell and back with no trouble, yet he had lost the undertaker out on land that boasted nothing more than being a glimpse of Hell.

He swiped at the river of sweat cascading down his forehead, dismounted, and tethered his mare outside the Prairie Dog Saloon. Considering his lack of money and the chance he had of earning more in Lost Soul, he pushed aside his thirst for a beer and drank instead from a water barrel sitting at the side of the saloon. He looked around before dunking his head in and getting some of the precious liquid into his mouth. Since the law thought it was trespassing to visit a whorehouse, stealing water left out for public use had to amount to a hanging offense.

This thought sent a shiver up Slocum's spine, in spite of the heat still radiating upward off the sun-parched ground. Anything Uriah Parsons said turned into a judicial order that got a man's neck stretched in this town. Slocum turned from the water barrel and saw Mrs. Parsons moving restlessly along the boardwalk, flitting from one hapless miner to another outside the saloon.

He shuddered again, thinking of her appetites and what it meant to whoever had to sate them.

For a hundred dollars Slocum did not want to be that man.

Purity Parsons found herself pushed aside when Marshal Webber came from the jailhouse and bellowed, "Gather round, you varmints. We got ourselves another hanging tonight."

Slocum let out a sigh of relief. He could see Silas Baker hanged and then move on; whether it was with or without Yvette didn't much matter to him at the moment, as long as he got out of Lost Soul. Seeing that thieving, backshooting Baker with a noose around his corrupt neck completed the picture, and then getting away from Lost Soul struck him as a worthy end to an otherwise dismal few weeks.

He sidled around the crowd, finding himself a spot to watch the execution near a dry-goods store long out of business. Slocum leaned back and made himself as comfortable as he could get. Baker might not have stood trial for the crimes he had committed against Slocum—and the money he had stolen was undoubtedly long spent or taken by Marshal Webber—but swinging was a fitting end to a miserable snake.

"We got a full card to offer tonight, folks," Webber said, a hint of enthusiasm coming into his voice. He might have been a sideshow barker beguiling people to buy snake oil or to come inside a tent and see miracles from lost civilizations. Slocum saw how the marshal appeared more eager, maybe even more competent. "Bring 'em on out."

Slocum blinked, thinking his day in the hot sun had doubled his vision. He had expected Baker and maybe one or two others. Six men were led from the jail, shackled together at the ankles. They shuffled forward and stood at the base of the triple-noosed gallows. One looked up, as if realizing for the first time what it meant to be executed. The rest stared at the ground, hoping for the entire nightmare to go away.

Slocum moved closer, pushing through a small segment of the crowd blocking his view. When he got a better look at the prisoners about to be executed, his stomach turned into a knot.

Silas Baker wasn't among them. Six men were going to have their necks stretched, and the man he wanted to see kicking in midair wasn't there.

"We got the full range of crimes to punish tonight," Marshal Webber announced in a voice as loud and confident as any caller at a square dance. "We got a killer, a man who cussed in church, and a sidewinder who, uh—" Webber hesitated, motioned over a deputy, and spoke rapidly to him. The deputy shrugged, went to where Purity Parsons stood, and spoke with the odious woman a few seconds. He cringed away from her wrath and hurried back to the marshal. A few more words were exchanged before the marshal continued.

"And we got a man who's guilty of not paying a bill owed our esteemed town patron, Mr. Uriah Parsons."

A murmur ran through the crowd. Slocum caught overtones of this being a crime many thought worse than murder. Still others cowered from the notion that crossing the town undertaker was all it took to hang. Slocum figured he knew the ones most likely to end up swinging in the evening breeze.

A loud commotion from down the street made him turn and crane his neck to see what was happening. He was not too surprised to see Parsons whipping his team viciously, forcing them to pull hard and fast after a day out in the hot sun. The buckboard bounced around, the wheels often leaving the ground, relieved of the heavy load it had carried earlier in the day.

"I'm here. You can go on with getting rid of these vermin," Parsons said. Purity Parsons joined her husband, her arms around him as if they were the most loving couple in the world. She rested her head on his thin shoulder, but her hot, eager eyes were fixed on the gallows. Uriah Parsons might bury the dead, but Slocum had the eerie feeling he knew who had really condemned these men to their deaths.

For different reasons, husband and wife applauded the executions.

Marshal Webber and his deputies worked on the chains and unfastened the first three nervous prisoners. They led the condemned men up the steps and positioned them on the trapdoors. Two continued to stare at their boots, as if finding salvation there. The third man struggled briefly until Webber got the noose around his neck. Slocum saw that the marshal was not using the black hoods usually placed over condemned men's heads.

A quick glance in Purity Parsons's direction told the reason. She wanted to see their faces as their necks snapped like dry twigs. An unholy monster, she devoured their fear like some toothsome portion of carrion left dangling on their skeletons.

Slocum expected some small ceremony, a pastor, a speech, a request for mercy, something. The clank of the trapdoors opening and the necks cracking like gunshots took him by surprise. Just as startling was the speed with which Uriah Parsons got the bodies down and laid out in the rear of his buckboard.

"Get the rest of them on the gallows," the undertaker ordered. The marshal hastened to obey. The next three were executed as quickly and ruthlessly as the first three. After Parsons and his wife drove off with the six corpses, the marshal went to the edge of the gallows and raised his arm to signal silence in the crowd.

"We got six more of them out of our town permanently," Marshal Webber declared. "We got more ready to be dispatched tomorrow evening, same time, same place. Y'all come back now, you hear?"

Slocum stared in disbelief. This was what passed for entertainment in Lost Soul. It certainly generated a considerable amount of business for the undertaker on a regular basis. Slocum wondered if Parsons made coffins in advance, knowing how many men were going to be executed in the coming month. Probably.

As Marshal Webber came down the gallows steps, Slocum went to the lawman.

"Quite a show tonight, Marshal," Slocum said, not bothering to keep the sarcasm from his tone. "You went and hung a bunch of outlaws."

"More to come, Slocum, more to come." Webber was obviously pleased with the night's work.

"How many do you hang in a month's time?"

"Three or six every other day till now. Pickin' up the pace, though, since the jail's overflowing with miscreants. We got to keep the peace in our fair town."

That explained why the population of Lost Soul was dwindling. Those that didn't have the good sense to leave were convicted on trumped-up charges and hanged for the amusement of Uriah and Purity Parsons. What it didn't explain was the hold of Uriah Parsons over the townsfolk. Fear often bred desperation. Any three or four men could waylay Parsons and his wife and be done with the despot running their lives.

Even assuming the armed men patrolling the Valley of Spirits worked for Parsons, the citizens of Lost Soul outnumbered them, Marshal Webber and his deputies, and the constantly armed Uriah Parsons.

Memory of the strange blood-red liquid Parsons had forced Yvette to drink came back to puzzle Slocum. It all had to be tied together, but he couldn't figure it out.

"Surely does keep the town quiet," Slocum observed, looking down Lost Soul's main street and seeing only a few men scuttling around like rats hiding from torchlight.

"Best town I ever marshaled in," Webber declared. He tipped his head a little to the side and asked, "You find yourself a job, Slocum? We don't cotton to deadbeats here."

"I still have enough money to keep me from being indigent, Marshal," Slocum assured him, worrying that the lawman was going to call him on the amount.

"Don't go getting into any games of chance, Slocum. Gambling is illegal in Lost Soul."

"Thought as much," Slocum said, interested in leaving as fast as he could. He headed down the street, turned between two buildings, and waited to see if Webber trailed him. When he was sure the marshal had gone about his business elsewhere, Slocum made his way back to the jail and the barred window where he had seen Silas Baker before. Peering in assured him Baker was still inside and alone.

The backshooter and thief looked up. A slow smile crossed his face.

"You come to get me out, John? It's about time."

"When are you due to hang?" Slocum asked. "I thought you were on the main bill for tonight."

"Not yet. Soon. Parsons is working up to me. I'm a big catch for him and that tinhorn marshal. You figure out how to get free of this town yet, John?"

"I wanted to see you dead before I headed on to greener pastures."

"There are armed patrols out there. Nasty sidewinders, and good shots too." Baker squinted a little as he studied Slocum's face. "So you *have* seen them! Then there are Parsons' armed guards at the mouth of the canyon. Beyond them, the Arapahos are always riled something fierce that their sacred land is being desecrated. You'll never get past any of them."

"But you know another way out," Slocum finished. "How'd you come about this information when you were less than a week ahead of me getting to town?"

"I stayed real busy. There are silver mines all over the hills. Thousands of ounces of silver are being pulled out of the rock."

"Guessed as much."

"I *know* as much. I've seen the shipments out of this valley. That's how I know there is another way free of this damned place." Baker turned bitter now. "You don't need to see me hang, not if it means you die too. Get me out of here, and we'll go skipping away scot-free."

"I got other reasons to stay."

"Some filly?" Baker spat. "There's not a one worth your life in this hellhole, even that skinny blonde at the saloon. You seen her show yet? Takes off danged near every stitch of clothing and stands there stark naked and all for Uriah Parsons."

Slocum tried to keep his face impassive. He failed.

"So she *is* the reason you're staying! You're a damned fool, Slocum. A damned fool. Forget her. She's already one of the town's namesakes, a lost soul. Walking around dead and she might not even know it, because there's more than one way to die here. Get me out and we'll hightail it out of the Valley of Spirits and the devil take the hindmost!"

"Don't go anywhere, Baker," Slocum said, walking off.

"Get me out of here!" For the first time, Baker's voice carried an edge of panic. Slocum counted that as a small victory. But it was a damned small victory. He went to find Yvette, only to find it was her night off at the Prairie Dog Saloon and the barkeep was proving especially tight-lipped about her.

Slocum stretched and got the straw out of his clothes. A drum boomed out in the street outside the abandoned livery stable, and a few notes from inexpertly played musical instruments made sure he did not go back to sleep. He wandered around the stable, wondering if the owner had left—or been among those being hanged the night before. The livery had been deserted since the first day he had come to town. For that, Slocum was glad. He appreciated having a free, secure place to sleep, even if he had been robbed of his bedroll the day before.

The noise grew louder, drawing Slocum to the door.

Down the main street paraded five miserable-looking men, blowing on trumpets and banging on drums. Now and then Slocum almost recognized the song they played. Almost. He settled his Colt Navy in its holster and went to see what the ruckus was about.

He watched the procession a few minutes, trying to remember where he had seen something similar. It finally occurred to him. Funerals in New Orleans were attended with laughter and music and a parade of friends and family as they carried the deceased to his eternal rest. This was a weird parody of those public rites.

Riding just behind the pitifully inept musicians came Uriah Parsons and his buckboard. In the rear of the wagon bounced six cheap pinewood coffins, the victims of the prior night's executions. The undertaker sat straight and proud as punch, taking in the crowd on either side of the street and waving as if he was some celebrity. Just behind him in the bed of the wagon stood Purity, smiling wickedly as they made their way out of town.

Slocum looked around to see if he could find Yvette watching the proceedings. She was nowhere to be seen. He edged along the street, then ducked into the cribs where she stayed, hoping no one saw him. Marshal Webber was likely to slap another trespassing charge on him, and this time Slocum wasn't likely to weasel his way out of it. The room where he had seen Parsons forcing Yvette to drink the dark-red fluid was empty. Even her pitiful bed had been cleaned out, probably thrown into the alley behind the building. Slocum went from door to door, hunting for someone who might know what had happened to the woman.

The building was as devoid of life as Lost Soul itself would be before much longer.

Slocum returned to the street and saw the funeral procession trailing behind Parsons's wagon. On impulse Slocum followed. It struck him as peculiar that the entire town had turned out, especially when most of them had given more than tacit approval of the executions the night before.

Slocum tried to engage several of the townspeople in conversation, but they edged away from him, letting him trudge along wrapped in his own somber thoughts.

Those thoughts were dark ones indeed. More and more he came to believe he had to save Silas Baker from the hangman's noose, not through any desire to see the man live, but because it might be his only way out of the valley. Slocum found it impossible to believe any of these fearful people would not have taken the first stage from town, if there had been a stage.

Uriah Parsons had the town bottled up tighter than the Arapahos, and Slocum might not have the time or luck to find his way free.

Still, Baker was not a trustworthy man. He might be lying just to get Slocum to break him out of the calaboose.

"Welcome, mourners, welcome, justice-lovers," boomed Uriah Parsons as he stood in his buckboard, towering above those assembled in the small cemetery on the outskirts of Lost Soul.

The undertaker acted as preacher saying words over the bodies of those he had railroaded into being hanged. Slocum found this ironic and more than a little frightening.

Parsons generated his own customers through the hold he had over the town. Sooner or later, though, he would have slaughtered everyone and filled the cemetery. Lost Soul would be a true ghost town. What then? Slocum knew finding out would mean he would have to be one of the last to leave the town, dead or alive. He decided to decline that singular honor.

Twelve men put their backs into digging new graves for the coffins and the contents. Slocum hung back, noting that many men slipped away, returning to town. By the time the graves were dug, only Parsons, his wife, and the grave diggers were left. Slocum hunkered down and partly hid behind a creosote bush, curious about what would happen next.

The twelve men were chased off, leaving Uriah and Purity Parsons behind. They wrestled the coffins from the buckboard themselves, setting them beside the narrow, deep graves. Slocum thought this was curious since the men they had sent back to Lost Soul were capable of lifting the coffins out of the buckboard, but then he saw the two had wanted a modicum of privacy.

When it became apparent they intended to make love atop the closed coffins before pushing them into the graves, Slocum knew it was time to find Yvette and get the hell out of town.

And if he couldn't find her and convince her to leave with him, he would break Silas Baker out of jail. Slocum doubted he needed the man's information, real or made up, about how to leave the Valley of Spirits. But he found himself wanting someone to talk to as he left who was not as crazy as a loon.

10

A mining town ought to have been alive, the streets filled with laughing men and drunk miners. Lost Soul's main street showed none of this bustling activity. The unpainted doors of the Prairie Dog Saloon stood open, pale yellow light spilling onto the dusty street in front of it. Only now and then did some patron inside cross the doorway and cast a fleeting shadow.

The entire town was like that. A shadow darting about, timid and fearful of any unusual noise. Slocum turned and stared at the three nooses blowing in the cold night wind. Six men had died there. Six men had met their maker to sate the bizarre appetites of the undertaker and his wife for death.

Slocum was reminded of stringy parasites growing on trees back home in Georgia. A little of the mossy Queen Anne's lace was attractive decoration, but too much killed the tree—and the parasite—by slow inches. That was the way he saw this town. Parsons and his wife were killing it day by day, and would eventually leave nothing but a husk of a ghost town behind.

Slocum turned and looked toward distant mountains ringing the Valley of Spirits. Somewhere out there was a silver mine that should have brought men and women rushing to

95

Lost Soul to make their fortunes. Slocum spat, thinking of Parsons waltzing away with that wealth. There was no one else in the entire valley likely to profit from those mines.

What was Parsons's hold over the people? They feared him more than being planted in the cemetery outside town.

"To hell with you, Baker," Slocum said, coming to a decision. Silas Baker could hang tomorrow or in a week. Seeing the man's demise mattered less to Slocum now than keeping his own hide intact. He had long since worn out his welcome in Lost Soul, making him a target of Uriah and Purity Parsons. They would order Marshal Webber to take him into custody and he'd end up hanging next to Silas Baker. That was not Slocum's idea of justice.

He passed the Prairie Dog Saloon and saw the usual arrangement of men inside drinking. Two stood at opposite ends of the bar. Three others had staked out their claims to tables in the corners of the saloon, protecting their drinks with cupped hands and looking around furtively, ready to run if anyone approached them. Slocum had seen cornered rats look more at peace with themselves.

The saloon held nothing for him. He stopped and stood in deep shadow as Marshal Webber and a deputy made a patrol down the center of the street. The marshal hunted for something—or someone. Slocum reckoned it could well be him after everything that had happened. He doubted the undertaker had spotted him spying on the strange tryst on top of the six coffins, but Purity Parsons had a temper and might have convinced her husband to lock up the nosy, uncooperative stranger.

Slocum heaved a sigh when the two lawmen circled the single line of buildings and headed back toward the jailhouse. He might be imagining things. Webber could be on a regular round to keep down trouble in this gravelike, silent town.

"The wicked flee where no man pursues," Slocum muttered, but he had no guilty feelings about anything done in town. He was right in fleeing rather than staying to be rail-roaded up and onto the gallows.

The one thing Slocum felt a pang over was Yvette and the notion of abandoning her. She had looked so alive when he promised to take care of her and get her out of Lost Soul. He made sure Marshal Webber had vanished before crossing the street to the doorway leading into the narrow hallway where Yvette had been. He spent more time this time going through her room, using every bit of his skill to find clues. That there was no trace of blood hinted that she had left of her own accord.

Slocum sat in the small room, his back against a flimsy wall, and thought hard. The only place where Yvette might have gone that would feel secure to her was the abandoned adobe out on the road where they had met before. Slocum heaved to his feet, went to the stable, saddled his horse, and rode out of town, looking over his shoulder more than he liked.

More than the marshal, Slocum worried about the armed riders on patrol around the valley. They never entered town that he could tell, but acted as a private police force—or prison guards keeping their wards bottled up. The ones not riding around stood guard at the mouth of the canyon lead-ing from the Valley of Spirits—he remembered them all too well.

Dismounting a couple dozen yards away from the burned-out adobe, he tethered his horse and advanced on foot. Slocum found himself growing more cautious the longer he stayed under Parsons's thumb. And that was not necessarily a bad thing.

He stood stock-still and listened hard when he came within a few feet of the adobe. Sobbing sounds alerted him to where Yvette had gone to earth. He swung around the doorway and saw her huddled in the corner of the building, legs drawn up and face pressed into her knees. Her entire body shook with the effort of not bursting out bawling.

"You don't have to stay," Slocum said. His words caused

the startled woman to jerk back, slamming hard into the baked mud-brick wall. She grabbed for a pointed stick at her side to use as a weapon. Yvette lowered it when she recognized him.

"I wasn't expecting you, John," she said.

"Why did you come out here?"

"I . . . I couldn't stay in town anymore. I just couldn't."

"Get your belongings. I decided not to wait to see Baker swing. This time we get through, then steal a couple Arapaho ponies. Don't much like the idea of having to leave behind my mare, but we can't get past both Parsons' sentries and the Indians on horseback."

Moonlight slanted down, turning her golden hair into quicksilver. Yvette shook her head, causing stray strands to rise like a ghostly mist around her head.

"No, John, I can't go. You don't understand how it is. I can't leave with you!" Her voice threatened to break with hysteria.

"You don't have to be afraid of Parsons any longer, not with me here." He moved closer, knelt, and put a hand on her trembling shoulder. Yvette's blue eyes were wide with fear. She calmed a little as he soothed her as he might a frightened colt.

"I know you mean well, but there's more here than you can ever understand," she said. "I want to go with you, I do!" She sniffed hard and wiped away the tears still trickling from the corners of her lovely eyes.

"Then do it!"

"No!" The single word carried all her fears and insecurities wrapped up in it. Slocum found himself alternately feeling sorry for her and hating her for being so weak. She returned his gaze and read his thoughts accurately.

She threw her arms around his neck and pulled him close. Slocum stayed beside her for a while; then she turned her face to his, her breath coming warm and gentle now that some of the fright had passed. She moved closer still and kissed him gently.

The kiss deepened into one that carried all her hopes and fears, all her passions, all her being. Slocum returned the kiss in kind until Yvette's ruby lips parted slightly and her tongue snaked out, darting about and lightly caressing his lips and tongue.

"We can do this after we get out of the valley," he told her. Slocum wanted to be on the way while it was dark and the chance for sneaking past Parsons's sentries was greatest. Pushing on past the Arapahos was another matter, and might take several days of careful movement, but the armed guards bothered him most at the moment.

"Hush," she said, silencing him in the best way possible. Her mouth worked against his. Slocum had thought her passion was unbridled before. Now it knew no bounds. The sexy woman pressed her body against his. They slowly reclined onto her thin pallet. Through her clothing Slocum felt the rubbery points of her nipples hardening. She stroked across his belly and lower until she found that part of him growing harder also.

With one hand, she skillfully unbuttoned his fly and released his raging manhood. Quickly snaring it in the circle of her fingers, she began a slow movement up and down that sent lightning bolts of desire lancing into his loins.

"We—"

"We have to do this now, John," Yvette said. She kissed him into silence again, then worked her way down his body. Here and there she unfastened his shirt with her lips and agile tongue, and then she reached his groin. Her mouth opened just enough to take him in. Slocum gasped and all strength fled his body. He let the woman work avidly on his hard spire while he ran his fingers through her long blond hair, stroking and guiding her in a way to heighten his own pleasure.

But that seemed greedy after a spell. He pulled her up so he could unfasten her blouse. Her snowy-white breasts tumbled forth, turning into silver in the moonlight. For a moment it struck him as odd that the only times they had made love were under the cold, hard moon. But perhaps that was fitting.

There was nothing hard or cold about Yvette and her trim body. He stroked over her delightful twin mounds of flesh, then sucked one bright pink tip into his mouth and gave her a measure of the enjoyment she had already given him. He bobbed from one to the other, licking and sucking, kissing and using his teeth enough to send shivers of delight throughout her body.

"More, John, I need more," she said in a husky voice.

"So do I," he acknowledged. He moved her body so she lay flat on the pallet, then hiked her skirts and found paradise. Her slender legs parted wantonly for him, revealing a furred triangle that promised to bring all their dreams to life.

He rolled over and moved easily, the tip of his manhood banging gently against her nether lips. Yvette fumbled for a moment until she found his pulsing stalk, then guided it directly into her fastness. They both gasped when he slid forward smoothly, easily, fully burying himself in her moist center.

"Yes, John, now, do it now. You're so big. A stallion!"

He felt as if he had been trapped in a collapsing mine. But instead of hard, harsh rock, he was completely engulfed by clutching warm female flesh. Her liquid core urged him to move. And he did, slipping back and forth easily. He began a slow stroking, building both their sexual tensions until sweat ran down Slocum's face and dripped onto the woman's heaving breasts.

He had been moving slowly to this point. Now his hips took over, as if they had a mind of their own. He began thrusting harder, deeper, faster. The friction along his length set fire to his passions. Yvette caught the urgency and gasped and moaned under him, her sobs far different now from when he had found her in this abandoned building.

He plunged full-length into her and rolled his hips

around. He felt her clinging softness clutch fervently at his hidden manhood. The heat in his loins grew to the breaking point as the white-hot tide of his release blasted forth.

Yvette arched her back and crammed her hips down to take him even deeper into her body. She cried out and soared like an eagle on the winds of ecstasy blowing through her. Then she sank back down. Slocum lay beside her, holding her, feeling the frenzied beating of her heart slow to a normal pace.

"I'm going to miss you, John. I am."

"Come with me. You don't have to stay in Lost Soul."

She shook her head. New tears formed in her eyes.

"You've got to go now, John. You have to, before it happens to you too."

"What are you talking about?" Slocum was puzzled. "Just ride out with me. Parsons won't be able to drag you back if you're with me."

"You can't understand, John, you can't," she cried. "Leave while you can. Without me. I have to stay here. I *have* to!"

Slocum sat up and glared at her, anger rising. Yvette refused to tell him what was going on, but if she wanted him to ride on without her, that was fine with him.

"Please, don't be angry with me. It's—" she began.

"Don't bother trying to explain," Slocum said, getting into his clothes and buttoning up again. He towered over her. She was still partly naked. And so beautiful in the moonlight. He couldn't remember a lovelier woman. Or one who could be so exasperating. "If you want to stay with that son of a bitch Parsons, do it. Just don't try to explain it to me."

He stalked off, as angry with himself as with her. He ought to pick her up, sling her over the saddle, and ride out, no matter how she complained. Promising not to abandon her ought to take precedence over her cowardice now.

"Good-bye, John," were Yvette's faint parting words. Slocum hesitated, then made his way through the darkness to where he had tethered his horse. The mare strained to graze at some sere grass.

"Come on," he said to the horse. "You're about the only one left in the world I understand." The mare turned a brown eye toward him, as if trying to figure him out. Slocum started to mount, but hesitated when he heard the rattle of wagon wheels along the road. He left the mare tied up and made his way to the road where he could watch from behind the cover of a mesquite bush.

"So, that's why she wouldn't go with me," Slocum said, his anger flushed out, replaced with only coldness. Parsons and his wife drove into view in their buckboard, making a beeline for the abandoned adobe. Yvette hadn't fled Lost Soul. She had come out here to rendezvous with the undertaker and his loathsome wife.

Slocum knew he ought to move on, but he wanted to be sure. After Uriah and Purity Parsons climbed down from the buckboard and went into the adobe where Slocum had left Yvette, he moved closer, peering through a large crack in the adobe.

What he saw turned his stomach. Purity was stripping off her clothes and beckoning to an unwilling but passive Yvette.

"Here, my dear. Here. Drink this, then drink deeply of what my wife is so freely offering!" Uriah Parsons handed Yvette a small clear glass filled with a bright blue liquid. This time, however, Yvette greedily drank it down without any threats needed. She drained the glass and handed it back to the undertaker.

"More, give me more."

"No, not now. Later. Afterward." Uriah Parsons indicated his grotesquely naked wife, now stepping forward and blocking Slocum's view of Yvette.

He had seen enough. Backing away, his gorge rising, Slocum returned to his horse and mounted. He couldn't get away from the Valley of Spirits fast enough now.

11

Armed sentries patrolled everywhere.

Slocum dismounted and went scouting on foot, only to find Parsons's men were far more alert than before. No longer were single sentries allowed to fall asleep on the job. Whoever commanded the guards had posted them in pairs tonight. Slocum saw one nudge his partner when he began getting sleepy, keeping four eyes studying the land toward the Valley of Spirits instead of two.

Or none.

Slocum realized he and Yvette had been lucky before in their escape attempt. He knew of no one else with enough grit in Lost Soul to try to sneak out, so this alertness meant he had poured boiling water on the guards' anthill. He was responsible for his own predicament. Sinking down where he could not be easily spotted, a rough granite boulder grinding into his back, Slocum considered his options. Nothing looked overly promising now.

"I've got to get through these pickets before even thinking about the Arapahos," he said to himself, idly drawing a map of the canyon in the thin dirt at his feet. Slocum tried to figure out the path, and decided skulking along one canyon wall was his best bet. The guards were posted toward the center, near the twin ruts that passed for a road leading into Lost Soul. If he cut across the roughest part of the canyon floor, he might avoid the guards and reach the outskirts of the gorge controlled by the Indians.

"How many can there be?" he thought. He had seen a gang of five or six armed men riding through the valley, but never more than that. Slocum knew Parsons to be a skinflint when it came to spending money. Anyone as greedy as the undertaker had to skimp on hiring gunmen, and those six might be all he had riding the range.

"I can get past six," Slocum said, returning to his horse. He took the reins and cut directly for the distant canyon wall. Stumbling in the dark over fist-sized rocks, Slocum wanted to find refuge before dawn in a few hours. He could never get past Parsons's guards before sunrise, and at some point he had to leave his trusty mare behind. That hurt him, but losing a horse was better than losing his own life.

His feet hurting after an hour hiking, Slocum finally saw the dark stone face of a sharply rising canyon wall in front. He turned into the canyon, making his way slowly across the uneven floor. Less than ten minutes of heading deeper into the canyon brought him to a deep crevice that required him to head back toward the biggest concentration of guards in the center of the gorge.

Cursing, Slocum had started retracing his steps when he heard something. Or rather, he heard nothing. The night noises had suddenly vanished. Slocum froze, turned slowly, trying to figure out what had stirred to make the animal and insect sounds go away.

He heard nothing, but his nose caught the tangy scent of tobacco smoke on the gentle breeze meandering down through the canyon. Someone ahead of him worked on a cigarette. Making sure his Colt rode easy in his cross-draw holster, Slocum advanced, alert for any sign of burning coal at the tip of the cigarette.

He spotted it a fraction of a second after the smoker's partner spotted Slocum. Hell broke loose before Slocum could respond. Foot-long tongues of flame leaped from one guard's rifle. Leaden death whipped past Slocum's head, tearing a notch in the brim of his Stetson. He jerked involuntarily, then ducked, drawing his six-shooter as he took cover. More rifle fire drove him to keep down.

"We got him, Asa. We got 'im pinned down over here. Come give us a hand with the varmint!"

From the distance came a loud whoop of joy. "Old Man Parsons promised a fifty-dollar bonus for the head of anybody tryin' to get out this week. Don't you go killin' him till I get there!"

Slocum heard other sounds all around, telling him he would quickly be surrounded. If Parsons had offered that much money for him, he was a goner if he stayed there much longer. Knowing his six-gun wouldn't do much good at a distance, he returned to his mare and yanked out his Winchester from its saddle scabbard. He turned, levered in a round, and fired directly at the coal still burning in the distance.

He heard nothing from his target, but got an earful from the man's partner.

"He done kilt Springer. Shot him smack in the forehead!"

Slocum grinned without humor. He had eliminated the stupidest of Parsons's men, nothing more. He still had at least two coming in for the kill, and they were not revealing themselves to him as the dead man, Springer, had. He realized he had just used up the only luck he was likely to see this evening.

Slocum swung into the saddle and turned his mare's face back toward the Valley of Spirits. He might get around the lookouts' flank if they all converged on the spot where he had shot Springer. Once past them, he could gallop a ways, then reassess his position so he didn't ride smack into an Arapaho ambush.

He let out a whoop and holler when he spotted a dark shape moving on foot. Slocum aimed and fired, yelling, "There the varmint is! Get him 'fore he gets away!" He fired several more times at the guard, hoping his partners would turn on the man.

And for a minute, they did, until the guard shouted angrily at his partners.

"It's a trick, damn you. I'm Asa! He's got you shooting at me!"

Slocum spurred his mare forward, angling in a direction he hoped would take him around the guards. He had not gone a hundred yards when he realized they had not been duped. Either the gunmen behind Asa were too slow, or they had hung back to protect against such a tactic. Slocum found himself being driven back toward Lost Soul by a curtain of fire that appeared to come from a dozen different places in the rocks.

His head low and making no effort to return their fire, Slocum turned back into the Valley of Spirits and Lost Soul. He hated being run off this fast, but had no choice. The number of guards and their alertness had worked against him. Vowing not to underestimate his foes again, he found the twin ruts of the road to Lost Soul and started back.

His horse had fallen into an easy trot when she suddenly broke gait. At first Slocum thought the mare had stepped into a hole or a stone had turned under a hoof in the darkness. But when she went down, her chest crashing into the ground, he barely got out of the saddle in time to keep from being pinned under her weight.

Snaking along on his belly, Slocum got back to the horse. The mare had died instantly when a bullet from behind had entered under her tail and gone plumb through her body. Anger mounted in him, but Slocum held it in check. Rushing back to avenge his stalwart mount's death would only get him killed too. From the sounds coming from far up the canyon, he might be facing more than a dozen armed and vigilant men intent on collecting the reward on his head.

Knowing he could not stay, Slocum patted the horse's

neck, then tugged and pulled until he got his saddlebags free. Tossing them over his shoulder, he dashed for cover among waist-high rocks down the road. He dropped to his knees, swung his rifle around, and waited to see if he could pick off any of the guards when they came down to see what they had killed.

Again Slocum was disappointed. They either suspected a trap or never knew that a stray slug had robbed him of his only friend in the valley. Slocum grew restive, knowing that the longer he stayed the better the chance the men after him had of circling and killing him.

Saddlebags once more over his shoulder, rifle in hand, Slocum started trooping for distant Lost Soul, an anger growing in him that would not die until he evened the score.

Slocum was half dead on his feet by the time he stumbled into Lost Soul. The sun beat down mercilessly, turning the entire valley into a deadly furnace. He had walked from the mouth of the canyon to town without so much as a sip of water. Finding the barrel at the side of the Prairie Dog Saloon was a gift he could never repay. Ducking his head into the barrel and trying to drink his way out only caused him to sputter and choke.

Pulling back, he flung water around like a wet dog as he shook himself. His eyes cleared to see a vision brought straight from Hell.

"Slocum," said Purity Parsons's grating voice. "I thought you might have left town. Glad you didn't. I need a big stud like you to service me. Come on over here and give me—"

"Burn in Hell," Slocum snapped. He remembered the sight of the detestable woman naked and advancing on Yvette—and the way the lovely blonde had permitted the obscene touches, all for a sip of Uriah Parsons's blue liquor. Although he hadn't eaten, Slocum's belly turned and tossed and threatened to lose what contents it had.

"You don't talk like that to me," Purity Parsons said, her eyes flashing angrily. Her bony hands balled into fists and rested on her hips. "You ought to know who owns this town and everyone in it!"

"You don't own me," he said.

The smile curling her lip looked to be almost a sneer. "I will. When I do, you're gonna suffer. You're gonna beg to be with me. Then maybe I'll let you. But only if you beg enough."

"I'll die first," Slocum said.

"That can be arranged," Purity Parsons said haughtily. She laughed in derision, cupped her thin breasts, and shook them in his direction. With that parting obscene gesture, she climbed the steps and went into the Prairie Dog Saloon. Slocum saw two men escape out the rear door. Another man, a miner from the cut of his clothes, wasn't as lucky. Purity Parsons led him like a leashed dog across the street toward the funeral parlor.

Slocum's hand rested on the butt of his six-shooter. He didn't much cotton to shooting anyone in the back, much less a woman, but for Purity Parsons he might make an exception. She was pure poison, evil to the bone, and a danger to everyone left in Lost Soul.

The woman vanished with her latest prey before Slocum could work himself up into enough of a state to actually throw down on her. He went back to drinking his fill of the tepid water in the barrel until he felt as if he might bloat. Thinking of that reminded him of his dead mare. Realizing that he had lost his best way of putting a lot of miles behind him sent a shudder through him. He was afoot and vulnerable unless he found another horse fast.

Silas Baker had bragged of knowing another way out of the Valley of Spirits. If Baker had found it in only a few days before being caught, that meant Slocum could find it. If he had a horse.

The thought again occurred to him that Baker could be lying, using this as a carrot to get Slocum to bust him out of jail. Somehow, Slocum did not think so. The man knew something—and Slocum could find out what it was without releasing the backshooting thief.

Knowing the livery was deserted, Slocum worked his way down the street hunting for someone who might have a horse for sale. He wasn't sure how he would pay for it with only two dollars riding in his pocket, but he could find a way. A promise to get the owner out of town when he went, perhaps. Slocum wanted to leave bad enough to promise almost anything to anyone.

Except to Purity Parsons.

"Caswell!" he called to the owner of the general store. The man looked around, as if hunting for a place to spit the half a worm he had just bitten out of an apple. "I want to talk to you."

"What makes you think I want to talk to you, Slocum?" the merchant said.

"I have a proposition. I need a horse and—"

Caswell turned without saying another word and went into his store. The door slammed behind him, the CLOSED sign was spun around, and the locking bolt rang out like a death knell. Slocum could not have received a more emphatic rejection short of a knife in the back.

He continued down the main street, asking anyone he saw about buying a horse. The reactions grew increasingly vindictive, until one man picked up a rock in the street and threw it at him. Slocum ducked, then reached for his six-shooter.

"Don't do that," Slocum cautioned.

"I'll kill you for what you done!" the man shrieked, going for another rock.

"What have I done?" Slocum asked.

"You got *them* riled at us. They're on a tear now, makin' life miserable for ever'one of us!" The man threw another rock, hitting Slocum in the arm. Slocum shoved his six-gun back into its holster and backed off. Killing the man might be a merciful thing, but it would also be cold-blooded murder.

As he walked away, the man started taunting him. This vituperation drew a small crowd of timid souls peering out of windows. A few of the more intrepid ventured out and joined in shouting insults at Slocum. He felt like turning tail and running—but there was nowhere to run.

He took refuge in the stables, sitting in the stall where his mare had chomped at hay only a day before. As he sat, he fumed. Purity Parsons had turned the entire town against him for refusing her sexual advances. Slocum spat like an angry cat, stood, and paced around, his hand occasionally touching the ebony handle of his six-shooter. There had to be a way out of Lost Soul.

No matter what trail his thoughts took, they always came back to Silas Baker's boast of knowing how to get out of the Valley of Spirits. Slocum got his back up and refused to consider breaking the man out of jail. Let the son of a bitch hang. There had to be a way out, horse or no horse, Parsons or not.

But what was it? Slocum came up blank.

Belly growling, he went hunting for food. The crowd had vanished from the bright sunlight, letting him roam the street unmolested. Slocum stopped in front of the café, only to have the door slammed in his face. Caswell at the general store provided no help. The Prairie Dog Saloon might have a sandwich to go along with a nickel beer.

It might have. Slocum never found out. The barkeep blocked his entrance, then closed the door without uttering a word. Slocum was left standing in the hot noonday sun, belly rubbing up against his spine and a thirst growing that the water left in the barrel at the side of the building wasn't likely to slake.

Slocum squinted into the blazing hot sun as he surveyed Lost Soul from one end to the other. A ticket on a stage-coach was entirely out of the question, there being no stage or railroad. Nowhere did he see an opportunity to buy pro-

visions, much less a horse. With so little money in his
pocket, he could hardly expect to buy a nag that wouldn't
die under him before he reached the city limits—or the
town cemetery. And finding anyone who would offer him
a job to earn money was out of the question. Purity Parsons
had spread the word around like a runaway prairie fire. He
was a derelict in Lost Soul even a leper would spit on.

"So what's it gonna be, Slocum?" came a lazy drawl.
Slocum spun, hand going to his six-shooter. At the end of
the walk in front of the saloon stood a man so gaunt he
would vanish if he turned sideways. His dark eyes were
sunken into black pits and his teeth protruded through flesh-
less lips. His neck was so scrawny Slocum wondered if the
man could swallow a pea—if the man had ever had a pea
to eat.

"Who are you?"

"Name's Eldridge. My friends call me Seth, 'cept I don't
have no friends left. I'm the new foreman at the mine."

"Met the last one," Slocum said, remembering with no
pleasure how he had killed Conrad by kicking him to death.
In spite of the former foreman's girth, the man had been
so fragile he had not put up much of a fight. Seth Eldridge
looked even frailer.

"Heard tell. No loss," Eldridge said, stepping up onto the
boardwalk. Every movement looked to be painful. He shuffled toward Slocum, stopping a few feet away. The man
carried the smell of death and disease about him. Slocum
wondered if the work in the mines had worn down Eldridge
to this point or if some avaricious disease ate away at the
man's enfeebled body. "You ain't gonna find no job in Lost
Soul."

"Figured that out all by myself," Slocum said bitterly.

"You want a job at the mine, you got it."

"Why?" asked Slocum, studying Eldridge's hatchet-thin
face for any trace of guile. "Why would you buck Purity
Parsons?"

" 'Cuz her hubby's even greedier than she is. He don't

care who mines his silver, as long as it gets pulled outta the ground. Pay's no good, but you get fed."

"I heard," Slocum said remembering Henry's tales of paying exorbitant prices for a single mouthful of water.

"Henry's got a big mouth. Always had. You wouldn't be workin' with him."

Slocum did not ask why not. Henry had probably gone the way of Conrad and so many others in Lost Soul. Slocum had not seen him since that day when Henry had told him he had been fired.

"It's not only the best offer you'll get," Eldridge went on, "it's the only one."

Slocum had no choice. He agreed.

12

Slocum saw the world through a heat shimmer worse than the middle of any summer desert. He wobbled on his feet, fought to keep from toppling over, then gave up and sank down on his heels. Staring ahead, he saw the small ring of daylight in the distance. He wiped at rivers of sweat and wished he had some water, but he had already used his quota for the day and he was damned if he would pay Uriah Parsons two full day's wages for a single dipperful.

"Get to work," barked Seth Eldridge. "You're not gettin' paid to take a siesta. You only been in the mine for ten hours. You got two more before chow time."

Slocum's belly tried to flip over at the mention of food. The victuals they passed off as edible would make a vulture puke. The twelve-hour days were bad, the food was worse, but the part that wore him to a nubbin was the lack of water.

"I need water."

"Water boy'll be around in a spell," Eldridge said. "You got the money to pay for him?"

Slocum shook his head, his resolve hardening. He would die before he paid Parsons a single dime for what ought to be a man's due in these murderously hot silver mines. He forced himself to his feet, staggered a little, and got a sec-

113

ond wind. Lifting his rusty pick, he let gravity do some of the work as the dull iron tip dug into the ore-laden wall of the mine.

He bent forward, as much in exhaustion as to pry loose the hunk of ore. A good-sized chunk fell to the floor where another miner would muck it later. From what Slocum could see, they were gnawing away at a decent vein of silver. The surrounding quartz was hard enough to need blasting, but Parsons either didn't want to spend the money for dynamite, or didn't trust his men not to use it against him.

Or both.

His muscles long past aching, Slocum fell into a mechanical motion of lifting, dropping, and prying loose that made it seem he was making progress. Eldridge grumbled and then moved on to spur other, weaker miners to more enthusiasm for their work. Whatever Eldridge was getting paid, it was too much. If Slocum had had the strength, he would have used the pickax on the man's skull-like head.

He laughed to himself. He was so tired, he might not be strong enough to drive the tip into Eldridge's hard head.

"Listen up, you slackers. We ain't payin' you to sit around on your asses. The boss says there's not been enough high-grade ore comin' outta this hole, so he's uppin' the quota. Everyone of you's got to produce an extra five hundred pounds of ore today . . . and every day from now on."

"What if we can't?" asked a man so thin he looked as though he would simply fade away if you looked away from him.

"Then you get that much cut back on your rations," Eldridge said. "Hey, you gents got it easy. *I'm* responsible when you don't dig enough. You know what it means if *I* don't make the nut every day."

Others nodded glumly, but Slocum spoke up. "*I* don't." He had thought Seth Eldridge a hard-boiled character capable of any cruelty to get just another pound of ore out of the mine—and the miners. He was startled to see a tear form at the corner of the man's eye and then roll down unashamedly, leaving behind a grimy, gritty track.

"He won't give me my due," Eldridge said. He swallowed hard, then bellowed at the men to return to work. Slocum was slow to obey. Eldridge's answer was no answer at all. As Slocum picked out the ore, he sidled down to the next man in the mine.

"What's he mean?" Slocum asked in a low voice. "Parsons won't pay him?"

The man looked at Slocum as if he had grown three heads. "We don't talk about it. Eldridge is no friend, but I wouldn't slow down to pester him. Wouldn't do that to my worst enemy."

"The blue liquid?" Slocum asked, taking a shot at the reason all the men were so frightened.

"Of course. What else?" The miner began loading ore into a wheeled cart pulled by four men in harnesses. Parsons used them like animals. No indignity seemed to have been overlooked in his contempt for them. Slocum had seen men wield power before, but not like this.

If an officer in the army got too haughty, his men had ways of removing him. They might misdirect their fire in battle just a mite. Only the stupidest of men failed to get the idea that they had more to fear from their own soldiers than the enemy.

Slocum had known a few, though, who had refused to take into account the men they led. He wished their fate could be shared by the undertaker.

The light at the end of the tunnel dimmed and Eldridge barked out that it was quitting time. There was no rush to leave. No one had that kind of energy. Shuffling like the half-dead men they were, the miners exited into a chilly twilight. The odors of cooking came from downhill, almost turning Slocum's stomach. Still, any food, even maggoty jerky, was better than none.

They filed past Eldridge, who had a stack of wood chips in front of him. He consulted a sheet before giving out the wooden markers.

"Slocum," Eldridge said, running his dirty finger down the list. "You made quota today. Here's for your food."

"You going to do this from now on?"

"No chip, no food," Eldridge agreed.

Slocum started down the hill on shaky legs as the man behind him in the line moved up.

"Dawkins," said the foreman. "Nope, sorry, you missed quota by damned near fifty pounds. No food for you till breakfast."

"But I'm hungry, Seth!"

"Next," Eldridge said. The foreman looked up, saw the pleading in Dawkins's eyes, and then shoved hard, sending the miner reeling. "Next!"

Dawkins moaned, but made no other sound. Slocum saw the man's pipe-stem arms and legs and protruding belly. He was about starved to death.

"Here," Slocum said, handing Dawkins his wood chip.

"I can't take your food."

"I don't feel up to eating that slop—not that the breakfast is any better."

"I can't," Dawkins said, but his resolve weakened. When Slocum thrust the wood chip into the miner's trembling, bony fingers, he almost broke down and cried. "I owe you, Slocum. Anything you want. Anything at all!"

"Forget it," Slocum said, knowing it was unlikely Dawkins would live long enough. Slocum looked around the ring of miners seated on the ground, gobbling at the pitiful supper as if the beef-flavored swill were good. He lounged back and tried to conserve his energy. He was hungrier than he could remember being in years, but he had not been in the silver mine long enough to be worked to an early grave.

"Early grave," he muttered. That had to be part of the picture in Lost Soul. Uriah Parsons loved being an undertaker, and any man dying in the mine got to be buried. Everything Parsons did showed his need for power. And who had the final laugh on a dead man but the undertaker who put him into the cold, cold ground?

Silver fed Parsons's greed. And the blue liquid somehow held the town in captivity. Seth Eldridge was fearful because of it, and Yvette refused to leave, no matter what Parsons or his wife did to her, because of it. The first bloody-red drink had been forced on her, but the second time she had been willing to do anything to get a drink.

What was the hell-brew?

Slocum found that he could no longer stay awake after the long day of backbreaking work in the mine. His eyelids drooped, and he fell into a deep, dreamless sleep, awakened later by the loud rattle of chains and the clatter of iron-rimmed wheels on gravel.

He rubbed his eyes and peered at the nighttime sky trying to determine the time. It was probably sometime past midnight. Slocum sat up in time to see a ghostly figure driving a buckboard up the road from Lost Soul. He did not have to make out the features to know Uriah Parsons was paying them a nocturnal visit like some Navajo skinwalker.

Slocum lay where he was and watched Parsons swing the buckboard around so it was near a shed fifty yards away, halfway between the mine and the crude smelter. Working in the mine was a better job than prying the silver loose from the ore using the noxious chemicals and blazing-hot furnaces. Slocum knew that men died turning the ore into bullion, numbering more than the miners who died.

He thought Parsons would call for Eldridge and get men to help him, but the undertaker always surprised Slocum. The hatchet-faced man rubbed his hands together, then set to work loading small silver bars from the hut into the buckboard. He chuckled to himself as he worked, and even sang out of tune. Slocum thought it was a funeral dirge, which might be as cheerful as Parsons ever got.

Slocum moved downhill, stumbling as he went. He

cursed his weakness. He had been in the mines only three days, and was already close to being debilitated. Slowing his advance, he drifted along like the night breeze and came up behind the hut. Peering around, he saw Parsons working steadily until the buckboard lattice sagged under the weight of the silver bullion. As Parsons worked, Slocum considered what he ought to do. A plan began forming, one with big holes in it, but better than staying to die in the silver mine. The heat would kill him within a week, if starvation or lack of water didn't take their toll first.

Parsons closed the shed door, used a tarp to cover his load, and then dusted off his hands and stood by the buckboard so that Slocum saw the evil leer on the man's face. Parsons then jumped into the driver's seat and snapped the reins. Slocum saw he had only an instant to make his decision.

Stay and die or go along and possibly die.

Three long strides brought him to the rear of the buckboard. Lifting the tarp, he jumped into the bed and lay down, hoping Parsons did not notice the extra weight. If the team did, they did not protest the heavier load they hauled. Slocum wiggled around so he could peek out from under the edge of the tarp. The last thing he wanted now was for Parsons to catch him.

The ride was bumpy, and Slocum felt as if his brains were knocked loose by the time Parsons turned onto a smoother road. This warned Slocum that they might be nearing a well-traveled section. He couldn't see where they were, but Parsons had driven parallel to the mountains forming the southernmost end of the Valley of Spirits, and now drove straight into the towering dark wall of rock.

Waiting as long as he dared, Slocum finally dropped off and hit the road. He staggered a few steps, turned, and saw Parsons driving on without noticing the change in weight. Slocum began hiking, trusting that Parsons would not look back and spot him. As he walked, Slocum's heart beat a little faster. The road was better defined than any other he had seen since finding Lost Soul.

Parsons—or someone—traveled along here often. From the tracks he made out in the dim starlight, only wheeled vehicles came along. Slocum knew he was heading for Parsons's silver cache. Gain control of it and he might get enough leverage to free Yvette from Parsons's savage control.

He caught his breath and held it when he topped a rise and looked down into an arroyo. Standing on the far bank was another shed, this one with a chimney pouring out a thin wisp of smoke. The odor of cooking food—real food!—made Slocum's mouth water. Parked to one side stood the buckboard. Parsons had not bothered tending the team. The two horses nervously pawed at the hard ground, obviously wanting free of their harnesses. Slocum moved to the side of the shack and searched the walls until he found a crack large enough to peer through.

Inside, Parsons wolfed down stew from a black iron pot cooking over the fire. Slocum blinked at the sight of so much food, but then when the lure of victuals faded a mite, he saw something curious. The entire wall of the shanty behind Parsons glowed a dull silver. It took him several seconds to understand why. Parsons had stacked up silver bars along the far wall so high, it was as if he had wall-papered the shack with it.

Slocum stared at tens of thousands of dollars in silver bullion. He had wanted a hold over Parsons. If he could hide the treasure trove, he would have it. Even as that thought crossed his mind, he dismissed it. Working for days wouldn't get this much silver hidden where Parsons could not find it. Slocum needed to get it far, far away and had neither the time nor the strength to do it.

The clatter of utensils on the table in the cabin brought Slocum back to reality. Parsons finished his meal, wiped his mouth on his sleeve, then opened the door and came outside. Slocum dropped to his belly and watched as Parsons unloaded the silver bars. It took him more than twenty minutes, but Slocum watched patiently, measuring his chance of overpowering the undertaker.

Slocum remembered the twin derringers in the man's shoulder harness. He might fall to Slocum's Colt Navy, if Slocum shot from ambush, but that was a course Slocum wanted to avoid, if he could. Backshooting was something a man like Silas Baker did.

Again Parsons surprised him. When the undertaker finished transferring the silver from the buckboard to the cabin, he vanished inside. The clack and clatter of glass rang out in the still night. Slocum returned to his crack in the wall in time to see Uriah Parsons mixing chemicals together in a large glass beaker. A clear liquid went in, then drops from a tiny bottle. The undertaker swirled the mixture around until it was the bright blue Slocum remembered seeing Yvette drink so greedily. His heart almost jumped up into his throat.

Parsons was giving him the way of getting Yvette free. He started around to the door, then hesitated when Parsons continued adding white powder to the mixture, swirling it around until it dissolved. Parsons crumpled the brown paper envelope from which he had poured the white powder and tossed it backhanded into the fire. A brief flare, and the paper was consumed.

Slocum hesitated now to stop Parsons. What was the powder? Obviously it was something important. And it was all gone. As he dithered, Parsons left the cabin, got into the buckboard, and rattled back down the road.

Slocum whipped out his six-shooter, cocked it, and lowered it slowly, taking aim on the undertaker's head. His finger tightened on the trigger; then he relaxed when he saw something beyond the undertaker. Parsons rattled up and out of sight, but Slocum forgot about the man.

"Baker, you son of a bitch. How'd you find this place?" Slocum wondered aloud as he made his way toward the rocky face of the mountains circling the Valley of Spirits.

Coming out of a mine shaft ran two rusty iron rails. Just in the mouth of the mine stood a dilapidated ore cart.

"Where does this go?" Slocum wondered, but he thought he knew. He had wondered why Parsons brought the silver to this deserted spot, but shiny steel wheels on the ore cart betrayed its recent use. "I'll bet you load the silver into the cart and push it all the way through the mountain. What's on the other side?"

He looked around and saw spoor from donkeys. Parsons might use them to pull the cart. Unlike the other mine where men toiled and died, Parsons had animals to do the real work here. Somewhere. Slocum scouted the area, thinking he might find a stable, but found nothing. The donkeys might be stabled at the far end of the tunnel—the tunnel leading out of the Valley of Spirits and to freedom!

Slocum headed back down to the cabin and went inside. The scent of stew made his mouth water. He finished what Parsons had left, feeling better for it. Then he poked around the glass jars to see if he could figure out what the blue liquid was. Parsons had taken all he had mixed with him.

Slocum hoped Yvette got her share. And even Eldridge.

He looked longingly at the wall of silver bars. Tossed carelessly on the floor he found leather pouches filled with silver nuggets, some the size of his thumb. The wealth in this room would let any man live like a king, but it wasn't enough for Uriah Parsons.

Slocum vowed to settle the score with the undertaker and his wife. Later. After he assured himself of his own freedom.

Hiking back up the hill to the mouth of the mine tired him, but the promise of getting away from Lost Soul lent strength to his legs. Slocum checked the tracks, assured himself the ore cart had been used recently, then started into the shaft. Less than a dozen paces brought him to a shelf holding a dozen miner's candles. He took the time to push a few into his pocket, not knowing how long he might be tromping through the mine, then used a lucifer to light a candle on a miner's helmet.

The flickering, wan light showed the mine going straight back into the mountainside for more than twenty yards. When Slocum reached the point originally at the edge of light from the candle, he saw another stretch—and four branching tunnels.

He knelt and studied each of the tracks going down the side tunnels, choosing the one with the most nicked track. Less than fifty yards down the tunnel he found a cave-in blocking the way. Retreating, Slocum went down another track, following it around the drift and marveling at the amount of iron rail dropped into this mine. But twenty minutes hiking brought him to another cave-in.

Slocum had burned through the candle, and replaced it with one of those he had stuffed into his pocket. As he retraced his path, he got turned around, and found himself walking in a section of the mine shaft that ended with a deep pit. He peered over the edge. The feeble light from his miner's candle didn't reach the bottom.

It took another candle burning to a waxen stub for him to return to the main juncture. He had guessed wrong twice. That left the largest of the remaining tunnels—and the one with the tracks in the most rusted condition—as the way through. Puffing and panting, his strength fading, he walked forward. This tunnel, like others, drifted about until he was confused as to direction.

Slocum came up against a solid block of stone where the tunnel ended. Marks on the wall showed some attempt at mining here had been done, but it had been long ago. The candle in in the miner's helmet burned down. He put in the last of the candles and wearily trudged back.

"What did I miss?" he wondered. The tracks snaked throughout the mine. Somehow he had missed a spot where silver had been unloaded and transferred. If there even was a way through anymore. Cave-ins might have blocked the escape route through the mountain.

Or it might never have existed. Baker might have been mistaken about this mine—or he might have found another passage out of the valley.

As Slocum began to hunt for proof there was no way through, his last candle sputtered and went out. He cursed his inattention in the dark and realized he was in no condition to hunt endlessly.

He started back to the mouth, hand on one wall to guide him in the pitch-black mine.

13

Slocum cursed as he blundered along through the darkness, beginning to worry he had taken a wrong turn and gone deeper into the maze of tunnels. Just as he began to despair, he caught a whiff of fresh air blowing in his face. Turning and turning again, he homed in on the breeze, and soon found a dim outline of the mine mouth. He heaved a sigh of relief and headed for it, bumping into the shelf with other miner's candles on it as he passed out into the night.

The stars had never looked bigger or brighter, even in Texas.

He sank down and rested a spell, thinking hard about what he was going to do. In his gut he felt this mine provided a way out of the Valley of Spirits. The evidence of donkeys inside told him that the animals had been used to pull an ore cart laden with silver bars to some other destination. Why hide them inside the mine?

The only answer to that question lay in the shack with its wall of pure silver. Uriah Parsons stacked the bars there until he had time to make the trip through the mountain to the other side. What lay there Slocum did not know. Probably another town, one the undertaker had not blighted with his eagerness to bury all the citizens. Maybe he had an accomplice who came through once or twice a month and carried the silver back.

Slocum doubted that. Parsons was too greedy, and greedy men saw treachery in everyone else. Whatever fetching and toting and hauling was done, Parsons did it himself. Maybe he went through the labyrinth of tunnels, got the donkey, and came back for a cart filled with ore. That kept him from stabling the animal on this side of the mountain.

"How long has it been since he made a trip?" Slocum wondered aloud. That was a powerful lot of silver in the shack. It was the wealth of a lifetime, yet Slocum felt it was only a few months' output from the silver mine where he had broken his back for too many days.

Slocum shoved himself erect and walked back to the cabin. This time he poked around, hunting for provisions. He found a small box filled with food at the corner of the single room. He had been so bedazzled by the wall of silver bars he had overlooked it before. Also overlooked was the canteen filled with fresh water. Slocum drank his fill, belched, and drank some more. The feel of water running over his tongue and down his throat was better than any whiskey.

He paced around, came to a decision, and picked up the leather pouch filled with silver nuggets. Slocum tucked this into his belt, then began fixing a pack laden with food from the box. Finding his way out of the Valley of Spirits did not look too promising at the moment, and the decision to free Silas Baker from jail did not come easily, but Slocum was willing to live and let live.

Especially if he could live with even a small portion of the fabulous wealth in silver in this cabin.

He set out walking along the well-defined road, and stopped and hid at sunrise, sleeping through the day to avoid the roving patrols Parsons had scattered throughout the valley, then continued his trek, reaching Lost Soul a couple hours before midnight.

The first place Slocum headed to was the livery. Abandoned as it was, he used it as his headquarters, stashing all but a few of the silver nuggets under the hay. From there he went hunting for a horse. Pickings were slim in Lost Soul, but he found a sorrel that let him pat its nose and steal it. Slocum left the silver nuggets as payment. Only when he had the horse secure in the livery did he head toward the jailhouse and Silas Baker.

If the man had not been hanged yet.

Slocum had been gone from town almost a week. From what Marshal Webber had said, he'd intended to swing Baker within a day or two of the six hanged before Slocum's last futile attempt at leaving the Valley of Spirits.

Cautiously approaching, fearful he might be too late, Slocum went to the barred window and peered in. He let out a gusty sigh when he saw Baker sitting on the bunk, head in his hands.

"You're not looking too chipper tonight," Slocum said. Baker jerked around, eyes wide. He leaped to his feet and rushed to the window.

"You've got to get me out, Slocum. Please!" the man begged. "They got me scheduled to hang tomorrow. They've gone through ten others. Ten men with their necks stretched! They're butchers!"

"They're crazy as bedbugs," Slocum said. "And I'm just as crazy, even thinking I ought to free you from jail."

"Please, you've got to!" pleaded Baker.

"Do you know the way out of the valley? Other than retracing the path through the canyon?"

"Yes, but I'm not foolish enough to tell you. If I did, you'd leave me to hang!"

"See you in Hell, Baker," Slocum said, turning and walking away. He forced himself not to look back to check Baker's reaction. As he turned the corner, he heard the man's frantic cry.

"I'll tell, I'll tell!"

Slocum ambled back, feeling a glow of success. He

stopped and stared at Baker, trying to gauge the man's honesty. Frightened of dying, Baker might actually forget to lie.

"There's a cabin out on the edge of the valley. A mine. An old mine. There's a way through the tunnels to the far side of the mountain."

"You seen the way through or are you just guessing?"

"Guessing," Baker said reluctantly, "but that damned undertaker vanished into the mine and didn't come out for hours. He wasn't in there working. I think he hightailed it through."

"But you never went through yourself?"

"No, but how hard can it be? I *saw* Parsons vanish into the mine."

"He have an ore cart loaded down, one pulled by a donkey?"

"A mule," Baker said. "And when he came back, he was pushin' the cart and that long-eared mule was gone. Why'd he leave it inside the mine? I never thought of that. He must have left it at the other side!"

Slocum nodded. This matched what he had surmised.

"You—you're gonna get me out of here? Tonight, Slocum, please, make it tonight. I'm going crazy with fear in here!"

Slocum stared at him. This was the man he had ridden halfway across Nevada to kill. Baker had robbed him and tried to shoot him in the back. The man deserved to hang, but Slocum felt a growing kinship with him. They were both trapped in Lost Soul. Maybe working together they could get free of Parsons and his wife.

"I need to make some arrangements. You're safe until tomorrow night. I'll have you out of here before then."

"Slocum, please!" whined Baker. "I've never seen a cell so secure. You got to work to get me out. Parsons has men riding all over the valley, armed and willing to kill anyone they find. There's a bounty on everyone they kill."

"Fifty dollars," Slocum said, remembering the exchange in the canyon.

"You know. Then—"

"Settle down and be ready for anything," Slocum said. "I'll get you out. I promise."

"Slocum! *Slocum!*" cried Baker as Slocum left. He had no real need of the man's cooperation, having heard confirmation of a path through the confusing maze of mine tunnels, but he had given his word. Baker's word might not be worth spit, but John Slocum's was.

Webber kept a close guard over the jail and its soon-to-be-hanged contents, so Slocum knew he needed help to create a diversion. The only one in Lost Soul he trusted even a fraction was Yvette. As he walked, he reflected on how he knew next to nothing about a woman he had made love to twice. He did not even know her last name, nothing much about her except she eagerly sought the blue liquid Uriah Parsons mixed up in the cabin out on the rim of the valley. Slocum wished he had brought a supply of the liquid with him, but Parsons had taken all he had mixed.

Slocum considered hunting for Yvette in the adobe at the other end of town, but thought she might be in the Prairie Dog Saloon, considering the crowd that had gathered. Men milled around on the boardwalk outside the saloon, but did not appear to be interested in anything inside. That made Slocum believe Yvette wasn't there. Even men in Lost Soul would not be indifferent if she did her dance again.

"There!" went up the cry from the end of town. "There he is. He's a'comin'!"

This brought people boiling out of buildings and into the dusty street. They pressed so close together Slocum could not see what the ruckus was over. He went into an abandoned store and climbed the rickety stairs to the second floor. From the upstairs window he had a good view of the street, even if he thought he was seeing a mirage.

Slocum shook himself, then told himself the sun had set hours earlier and it was now downright cold in the desert town. Mirages never showed themselves after dark, in the chill, when a man was rested and fed and watered. But that was about the only explanation for what he saw coming down the street.

Like some Chinese potentate, Uriah Parsons rode in a sedan chair decorated with gold tassels, precious stones, and hangings that might have been Persian rugs ripped off some floor. Struggling with the sedan chair rails were four gaunt men, starved almost to death, but gamely staggering along. As they passed under his vantage point, Slocum heard Parsons bark, "Smoother, you fools. Give me a smoother ride!"

The undertaker used a short whip on the men in front to force them not to bounce him about as much. One visibly weakened and stumbled. Rather than spilling Parsons to the ground, four other men from the crowd rushed up, each vying for the dubious honor of carrying Parsons along. To Slocum's utter surprise, the man who had been whipped and had staggered fought to keep his post. Parsons used his whip to drive the man away, allowing another, stronger volunteer to take his place.

"There," Parsons ordered imperiously. "Place my throne *there*." Using his whip, he pointed to a spot in front of the funeral parlor. The four men turned the sedan chair around and set it down gently, then fell to their knees in place.

"Good, very good," Parsons complimented them, like a hunter might do with a bird dog in training. Slocum expected Parsons to pat the men on their heads. Instead, he did something even stranger. He fumbled in the piles of pillows around him to pull out a large clear beaker of the bright blue liquid. This caused a surge in the crowd. They raced forward, only to stop in their tracks when Parsons held the beaker out to one side and made as if to pour it into the thirsty dust.

"Stay back. *I* decide who is to be rewarded. These four," he said, indicating the men who had acted as his bearers. "Here!" Uriah Parsons held out a small shot glass and filled it. The four men pushed and shoved for their chance to down a small portion of the liquid.

"Please, Mr. Parsons, please. I carried you all the way into town," begged the man who had flagged at the last minute. The skeletal man was on his knees, hands clutched as if praying. "I deserve some!"

"A shot to the man who kills him," Parsons said, glaring at the kneeling man. The stricken man's eyes went wide; then he was driven to the ground as men pummeled him with their fists and kicked at him with their boots.

Slocum's stomach turned when he saw one man use his spurs on the fallen man, now probably dead. It did not seem to matter. The lethargic crowd had been galvanized by Parsons's flashy entrance. Now they showed more energy than at any time since Slocum had come to Lost Soul while carrying out the undertaker's vicious order to murder.

"Good, good," Parsons said, sneering. He pointed to the man using the spurs and one other. "You two. Here!"

They fell over themselves getting to the undertaker's feet to accept the small drinks of blue liquid.

"Thank you, thank you," gushed the man with the spurs. Slocum's fingers tapped on the ebony handle of his six-shooter, considering how easy it would be to remove this vermin. But he wondered if the vermin wasn't being driven by Parsons's cruel desires.

"You, you, and you!" cried Parsons, picking men at random from the crowd, giving each the taste of his blue liquor. Hands shaking, overly eager, each took the drink and profusely thanked the undertaker for his generosity in dispensing the drink to them. It made Slocum even more curious as to the substance. He had watched Parsons mix it in the cabin, but the only portion that remained a secret had been the white powder from the envelope the undertaker had tossed into the fire. All the other ingredients were on the shelf in the cabin with the wall of silver ingots.

"No more," bellowed Parsons. The crowd turned ugly. Marshal Webber and his deputies moved in, using their ax handles to drive back the irate citizens of Lost Soul. The marshal looked expectantly at the undertaker, and was rewarded with a small sip of the blue liquid, as were his deputies.

Then Slocum watched in utter disbelief when Parsons said, "Drinks for sale now. Fifty dollars."

The finest brandy Slocum had ever sampled, the best champagne, the smoothest whiskey, had never sold for such a princely sum. Slocum thought Parsons was only taunting the crowd, that no one would buy. He was wrong. Men haggled among themselves, pooling their money so one could buy a drink. Slocum wondered at what was promised by the lucky recipient of the drink to the others.

He really did not want to know.

Slocum had started to leave his vantage point when he spotted Yvette at the edge of the crowd. She made her way toward Parsons, moving at first with great deliberation and then with greater urgency until the fear on her face radiated like the sun itself. The blonde reached the point of clawing her way through the crowd to get to the front.

She threw herself to her knees in front of Parsons and grasped his arm. He jerked free and raised his whip, then saw who had accosted him.

"Please, Mr. Parsons, it's been too long. I need it, I *need* it!"

"Of course you do, my dear." Parsons did not stop selling the shot glasses filled with the blue liquid. When he got down to a single remaining ounce in the bottom of the flask, Parsons swirled it about, looking from an openly crying Yvette to the crowd. A sneer curled his lips.

"A bid! Who will be the highest bidder for this last drink of elixir?"

Slocum was stunned when a man offered three hundred dollars and was given the shot glass by the undertaker. Every last drop had been drained from the glass bottle— and Parsons handed it to Yvette. The woman grabbed it and tongued the rim, trying to get nonexistent drops out of the flask. She sagged when it was apparent to everyone watching that she had not even wetted her lips, much less gotten a real drink.

"My dear, come closer," Parsons beckoned. Yvette sidled closer. The undertaker held her in a most obscene manner and whispered in her ear. Yvette listened, then tried to back away, her face a mask of horror. Parsons held on for a moment longer, then released her.

"Please, no, I can't."

"Of course you can," Parsons said, gloating. "And you will, if you want more."

"I beg you!" Yvette grabbed Parsons's hand and pressed it to her cheeks. He jerked away.

"Your choice." Parsons settled back in his sedan chair and waved indolently, dismissing the masses. His four carriers hefted the shafts and started him out of town again. The crowd murmured in discontent, but Slocum could not take his eyes off Yvette. She was a huddled, defeated woman, bent over in the street next to the marks in the dust where Parsons's sedan chair had been only minutes earlier. Slocum had seen shattered men during the war, men tortured by the Apaches, men broken emotionally by hardship and loss, but never had he seen a human being as defeated as Yvette.

He ought to have killed Parsons when he had the shot, but he told himself he might have been mobbed and killed. The people of Lost Soul kowtowed to the undertaker as much as they hated him. Slocum did not understand. But he would.

14

Slocum went to the street and mingled with the slowly dispersing crowd, trying to listen to their comments. All he caught were curses about bad luck, vague claims to be worthier and to be in the front of the line next time to get a portion of the blue liquid, to do all the things that perplexed Slocum so much. Everyone feared Parsons, but no one voiced the opinion that they ought to kill the son of a bitch.

The souls in Lost Soul truly were that—lost.

Slocum hunted for Yvette, but the woman had hurried away after Parsons had whispered his instructions to her. Whatever he had said had horrified the blonde to the point where she had blanched and argued. But like the others in town, Yvette had finally acquiesced. What *was* the undertaker's hold over the citizens in this town?

A small stream of men drifted toward the Prairie Dog Saloon, so Slocum followed. Finding Yvette if she chose to hide out would be dangerous for him. Marshal Webber had to be hunting him if word from the silver mine had come that Slocum had vanished. While men undoubtedly died all the time there, they always got planted by the undertaker. No body, no funeral meant true fury on the part of Uriah Parsons.

Slocum had been in a prison or two in his day, and the

men silently filing into the saloon looked like long-term prisoners. They kept their eyes on the ground, avoided contact with anyone around them, not jostling or joking, and shuffled their feet as if they had been beaten into submission. Before the war, Slocum had seen slaves with more spirit.

This despondency worked for him. No one glanced in his direction, as if this would bring them unwanted attention. Slocum had a few silver nuggets in his pocket, but chose not to use them to buy either beer or whiskey. Instead, he found a secure place in the far corner of the saloon where he could watch the forlorn crowd nursing weak drinks and trying to be as far from their neighbors as possible. What worried Slocum was the chance Webber might waltz in with a few of his deputies and cause a ruckus that Slocum would have to shoot his way out of.

But the law remained outside on patrol, doing whatever it was they did other than guard the prisoners in the jail. In spite of the dearth of tin stars, Slocum felt a rising tension in the crowd, as if a dam was about to burst. He settled down in a chair, each shoulder against a different wall of the Prairie Dog Saloon. Resting his hand on the butt of his Colt Navy, Slocum waited for whatever was going to happen.

He did not wait long. The piano player came out, cracked his knuckles, then began a carefree tune completely out of character considering the dour clientele. This did not stop the man from going into yet another song that was even livelier. Then the barkeep jumped onto the small stage at the end of the saloon, held up his hand, and made his announcement.

"Gents, we got a special act tonight. Miss Yvette's gettin' ready to perform a dance you'll remember till the end of your days, or so sez Mr. Parsons!"

This brought Slocum upright. He kicked away the chair so he could stand and crane his neck to get a better view. The piano player kept hammering away at his relentlessly cheerful tune as Yvette came out, dressed in her usual feather boa.

It took Slocum a few seconds to realize she did not have any clothing on under the slipping, sliding, constantly moving brightly colored feather boa. She slid it between her legs, exposing her privates as she turned. Her rump gleamed whitely in the light from the three kerosene lamps placed along the front of the stage and acting as spotlights. And her breasts! Even from the back of the room Slocum saw the coppery nipples, the white flesh, and the way they bobbed about as she tried to dance in time with the music.

Her dance was lackadaisical, and Slocum knew why. This naked dance in front of the miners and other men from Lost Soul could not have been her idea. Uriah Parsons had put her up to it—more, he had forced her to do it for his own sick pleasure.

Slocum's grip tightened on his six-shooter, then relaxed. He did not know what Parsons's hold might be over the lovely blonde, but she was giving in to his demands. Yvette could have told him off and left. She had chosen to humiliate herself in public.

"Very good, very, very good," called Parsons's grating voice. "You are so lovely, my dear. Everyone! Give Yvette a round of applause!"

The men in the saloon clapped. Slocum refrained from drawing and firing. He saw the fear in those men's faces—and in Yvette's. She was terrified, and he had no idea what it was driving her to this lewd public act.

Parsons strutted forward arrogantly, parting the few men bold enough to crowd closer to the stage to see Yvette's naked glory. For a moment, the undertaker did nothing but stand and watch from his vantage point next to the stage. Then he began clapping slowly, deliberately, mocking the woman's performance.

"Please, Mr. Parsons," she begged.

"Dance!" he ordered harshly. Parsons turned and cried, "Convince her to continue, boys. Clap, damn you, clap!"

Everyone but Slocum began clapping. His fingers tightened around the six-gun in his holster, but he needed to
know what hold Parsons had—and he wanted Yvette's help
getting Baker out of the jail. It would not do to raise a
ruckus bringing the law into the saloon, no matter how
satisfying it might be to kill Parsons now.

Three different tunes came and went through the piano
player's fingers, and Yvette danced naked to each. She
stumbled and staggered about, weak from effort and hu-
miliation, before Parsons put an end to it.

"I am going to reward our proud terpsichorean," Parsons
declared, making a big show of reaching into his pocket
and pulling out a silvered flask. The crowd in the Prairie
Dog Saloon went silent. The barkeep shoved over a shot
glass. Parsons smirked as he uncorked the flask and poured
two fingers of bright blue liquid into it.

"Back!" Parsons snapped when the crowd moved closer.
He turned and gave the glass to Yvette, who took it with
shaking hands. She upended the drink and drained every
last drop.

A curious mixture of relief and dismay passed through
the crowd. Slocum saw some were glad Yvette had had her
dubious reward. Others appeared angry that they were not
the recipients. Then all resentment vanished when Parsons
made his announcement.

"Divvy it up among the first twenty of your fine customers," Parsons said, sliding the flask to the barkeep. Slocum
saw the bartender take a drink himself before passing out
the liquid to the others.

Parsons laughed at their eagerness to drink, and ridiculed
them when they thanked him profusely. He left the Prairie
Dog Saloon the same way he had entered, strutting like the
cock-o'-the-walk.

Slocum ignored the undertaker and pushed his way past
those at the bar to reach the back door where Yvette had
gone. He had to talk with her.

He caught up with her halfway out of town, headed in

the direction away from the abandoned adobe on the other side of Lost Soul.

"Yvette!" He grabbed her bare arm and spun her around. Her cheeks were flushed, and she looked more alive than she had in his memory. She made some effort to hide her nakedness with the feather boa, then stopped, realizing it was a fool's errand.

"I thought you were dead, John. They said . . . at the mine . . . no one's ever got out of there alive."

"I want some answers. What went on back there in the saloon?"

Her lip curled slightly into a sneer. "You gone blind? It pleased the rest of the miners." Yvette stepped away from him and danced, her body moving sinuously.

"Stop that. I meant the blue fluid he gave you to drink. He forced you to dance like this to get the drink. What is it?"

"You should have left town, John. You had a chance."

He grabbed her with both hands and shook. Her head snapped about and she laughed, but there was no humor in it. "You're a fool to get involved," she said.

"Tell me what's going on. How does Parsons force everyone in Lost Soul to act like slaves?"

"Poison," she said.

"What?"

"He made me drink a poison—everyone, purty near, left in Lost Soul has drunk it too. It's a dark red, and he forced me to drink it at gunpoint. I didn't want to, but he would have killed me then and there. I should have let him shoot me. It would have been kinder."

"A poison?"

"And the blue liquid is the antidote—for a short while. If we don't keep drinking it, we'll die. Horribly. Better to be killed by the Arapahos maybe." She shivered, and it was not from the cold desert wind whipping through Lost Soul and across her bare flesh. Even talking about the poison made her restive.

"How do you know you'll die? Might be the son of a bitch is lying to you," Slocum said.

"No, no, it's a real poison. It burned at my throat and belly something fierce. I could hardly bear it, but I lived. Some don't. Some die then and there. But since I did survive, I don't want any more of pain like that if I can keep pleasing Mr. Parsons."

"The low-down, no-account, lily-livered polecat," Slocum began. He bit back more vituperation because it served no purpose. He took a deep breath. "Show me how this poison works, if you don't get the antidote regularly."

Yvette swallowed hard, then said, "There's a man in town who's refusing to do what Mr. Parsons says. Everyone knows he doesn't have much longer."

"Who?"

"Caswell, the owner of the general store. Ever since his boy got gunned down, he's been agitating about doing something."

"I want to talk to him." Slocum grabbed her arm and pulled her along behind like a reluctant child. They went directly to the general store. Slocum banged on the door, but got no response. He saw that a single light shone through the upper-story window where Caswell lived.

"There's a staircase on the far side of the building," Yvette said.

Slocum pushed the woman up ahead of him, then knocked hard on the flimsy door. When he got no answer, Slocum tried the doorknob. The door opened easily, showing a small sitting room leading to the bedroom. That door stood ajar, letting Slocum see Caswell on the bed. The low groans drew Slocum the way a lodestone pulls iron.

"Let him be, John. There's nothing that can be done for him now," Yvette said, her arms wrapped around herself.

Slocum knelt beside Caswell's bed and put his hand to the man's head. He was burning up with fever. He was sweating like a pig, his complexion pale and his face drawn.

When his eyes opened, they stared at—through—Slocum without seeing.

"What happened?" Slocum asked. "Are you dying from Parsons' poison?" He got no answer. Caswell gulped and made an attempt to pick up a cup of water from a table beside the bed. He was too weak. Slocum helped him, but the man never spoke, never gave any sign of knowing what went on around him. Caswell sank back to the bed after taking a few sips of the tepid water, and fell into either a deep sleep or a coma. It hardly mattered. Slocum had seen men near death before, and Caswell skirted as close as he could without actually passing over.

"The poison's got him. He crossed Mr. Parsons and was refused any of the antidote," murmured Yvette.

Slocum was not so certain. Caswell might have cholera from the symptoms. That was bad enough, maybe worse than being poisoned. The water supply in Lost Soul couldn't be well maintained, not if barrels were left outside for anyone to drink.

Or it might be as Yvette claimed. Slocum could not be sure.

"I need help breaking Baker out of the jail," Slocum said, backing off. If Caswell died from poison, there was no need to fear the body. If he died from cholera, Slocum wasn't so sure he wanted to be within a country mile of the place.

"No, John, I can't. He would let me die like Caswell. I—"

Slocum clamped a hand over Yvette's mouth and looked around for somewhere to hide. A wardrobe stood against the far wall. He pushed aside the few rags hanging inside and shoved her in, crowding in beside her and drawing the door almost closed. He peered out of the thin crack and watched Marshal Webber come in, followed by two deputies and Uriah Parsons.

"He's a goner, Mr. Parsons," said the marshal. "What you want done with the body?"

"A funeral, a fine, wonderful funeral, Marshal," declared

Parsons. The undertaker's eyes glowed in the dim light from the kerosene lamp on the table. He rubbed his hands together like a miser counting his gold as he stepped forward. "It will be regal, splendid, the finest this town has ever seen!"

"He don't have family to pay for it," Webber pointed out.

"Confiscate his store and everything in it. Sell it off to the townspeople. Raise the money. Lots of money for the funeral. What kind of coffin would look best with his facial structure? His hair color is off. We might dye his hair to look less . . . gray. Purity is good at such cosmetic improvement."

Parsons circled the bed, going from one side to the other, eyes fixed on Caswell's still-feverish, alive body like a vulture waiting for a wounded rabbit to die in the hot desert sun. Again, Slocum had the chance to gun down the undertaker, but could do nothing about it. He silenced Yvette.

"You want to put off the rest of the hangings till after Caswell's funeral?"

"No, not at all. We can do another mass ceremony in the cemetery. Purity likes them." Parsons cackled. "So do I."

The lawmen and the undertaker left then, Caswell moaning softly in his distress. Slocum pushed open the wardrobe door and climbed out, Yvette following.

"We've got to get Baker out quick. They'll stretch his neck by this time tomorrow if we don't."

"No, John, I can't. You saw what happened."

Slocum flipped between contempt for the woman and understanding her dilemma.

"All right, I'll do what I can by myself. Take care of yourself, Yvette."

He started out, but she grabbed his arm and clung tightly to him. She sobbed silently, then looked up, her bright blue eyes moist with unshed tears.

"You're the only decent thing in this whole damned town," she said. She impulsively kissed him.

Slocum wanted to do more for her, but knew she had to want to help herself first. He had other problems to tend to, ones requiring immediate solutions. He glanced out the door at the head of the stairs. Seeing that Webber had vanished into Lost Soul, he started down.

Heading for the stable, he paused, turned, and saw Yvette in the street. She waved to him, a curiously innocent figure in spite of her nakedness. He tipped his hat in her direction, then started for his stolen horse, a thousand plans racing through his mind. There had to be some way to free Silas Baker from the jail.

He was so engrossed in plotting and planning the jailbreak he neglected to pay enough attention to his surroundings. He rounded the front of the livery, and had put his hand on the locking bar to open it and go in when a cold voice from behind said, "You're a dead man if you move a muscle. I'm Deppity Baltimore and I got the drop on you, Slocum."

The distinctive feel of a six-shooter muzzle shoved into his spine emphasized how much trouble Slocum had fallen into.

15

A million thoughts raced through Slocum's mind, and none of them got him out of his predicament. He had been in tight spots before and knew the hot breath of death blowing down his neck. Never had that breath singed his flesh quite so much.

"Keep them hands where I kin see 'em," came the deputy's command. He sounded eager now, knowing who he had caught and anticipating the reward. That eagerness and greed might make him careless, if only for a brief instant. Slocum considered spinning, drawing, and firing blindly. He was not sure where the lawman stood. With the six-shooter shoved into his back, Slocum knew he was courting death—but better to die cleanly than to hang alongside Silas Baker or have Uriah Parsons force the vile poison on him.

As he tensed to make his move, Slocum heard a soft shuffling noise in the dust that he could not explain. Immediately after it came a *thwack,* a grunt, and the sound of a heavy man falling to the ground. Slocum spun about, his six-shooter clearing leather. His left hand came back to fan off a few rounds, but he saw this wasn't needed.

Yvette stood with her legs spread wide and planted securely, a long two-by-four in her hands. She had stopped the deputy's arrest in the best way possible, connecting the lumber with the back of his head as accurately as any baseball player hitting a pitch.

"Thanks," Slocum said, meaning it. He dropped to his knees and began tying up the deputy with a piece of rope from a nearby pile. Slocum realized then how foolish he had been, how old reactions had betrayed him. Lost Soul was about the only town he had ever been in where the law did not go armed. The deputy had thrust the end of his ax handle into Slocum's back, making him believe he had been covered by a six-shooter. Slocum wished the man had carried a pistol. He could use some extra firepower right about now.

"What are you going to do?" she asked.

"Get this one out of sight, then free Baker from the jail. I promised him." Slocum hoped he did not have to explain to her how stupid he had been thinking the deputy had gotten the drop on him with a six-gun. She seemed not to know what chagrin Slocum felt over this. She was too caught up in how she had leveled the man.

"You always keep your promises, don't you?" she said.

"You make it sound like a failing of mine." Slocum looked up at her and grinned. Yvette either had not realized he had invented the tight spot she had rescued him from, or did not care. He suspected the people of Lost Soul were so cowed by the lawmen and Uriah Parsons that she'd never wondered why he had not saved himself.

"No," the blonde said, smiling with some humor now, "I like it. It makes you different from 'bout every other man I ever met."

"One thing's for sure," Slocum said, dragging the deputy into the stable and fastening him down securely using more rope. He gagged him, although the lawman showed no sign of coming to any time soon. "I'm different from any man in Lost Soul."

Yvette moved to him and put her arms around his neck. She looked up at him. This time the fear was gone, replaced with something else. Slocum did not want to take the time to find out exactly what more it might be, but he had no choice.

"Kiss me," she said softly. He did. The kiss deepened and together they waltzed around the stable, dancing to a music only the pair of them heard. Somehow, as they moved together, bodies rubbing here and there, Slocum eventually became as naked as the blonde.

"This is better," she said, her hand on the hardness sprouting from his groin.

"No," he said, cupping her buttocks in his hands and lifting powerfully. Her legs spread wide and circled his waist. The purpled crown of his manhood touched lightly the lust-dampened nether lips, then sank deep into the woman's fiery core as he lowered her.

She gasped in reaction. Slocum found that his own response was about the same. He turned weak in the knees, and leaned back to support himself against one of the stalls. He started to speak, but Yvette's mouth engulfed his, smothered him with kisses, made any weakness a passing one for him.

With her strong legs circling his waist, his freed hands roamed up and down her smooth back. His callused fingers traced out each and every bone in her spine, causing goose-flesh to form as he passed up to her slender neck.

"Oh, yes, John. This is so good, so very, very good. I can almost forget—"

He did not permit her to linger on bad thoughts. He wanted only good. Twisting and turning under her, he drove himself deep and hard, touching hidden spots far within her fastness. Heat from the movement built and threatened to melt him. Slocum fought down the impulse to end this lovemaking too soon. Yvette was so lovely, so willing, so knowing. He wanted this to last forever.

Except it could not.

It was Slocum's turn to lose himself in the carnal treats offered by the woman to drive away the knowledge that

they were both trapped in Lost Soul unless he found a way
out of the valley.

Her naked breasts rubbed erotically against his chest. He
loved the sensation of the rubbery nipples dragging across
his body as he held her close. Yvette's hips began thrusting
downward, matching every move he made upward. They
twirled about each other, his hardness the axle about which
their world revolved. Yvette began gasping and moaning
and pleading for him to do . . . something. He could not
understand her, and would not have been able to oblige if
he had.

He was too far lost in the sensations ripping into his
body. The heat of her body, the heat of the friction of their
mutual movement, the tightness all around him—it all ig-
nited the powder keg hidden in his balls. The fiery tide rose
and then blasted the entire length of his shaft as Yvette's
most intimate recess tensed and squeezed at him.

Slocum stood upright and spun about in a circle, shoving
his hips upward in an attempt to drive even deeper into her.
Yvette's legs relaxed a mite, allowing her body to sink
down onto him. The dual motion gave them both more
pleasure, pleasure that sent them sailing far away into mo-
mentary forgetfulness of their plight.

All too soon, the muzzy feeling vanished and Slocum
wrapped his arms tightly around the blonde's sleek body to
lower her to the stable floor. Yvette sagged a little, supporting herself against his sturdy body. Then she pushed
back and stood on her own feet.

"I'll do it, John," she said. "But you have to promise me
you'll do what you can to find some of the antidote."

"Just some?" he asked, curious.

"I want you to get enough so we can get the hell out of
Lost Soul and the Valley of Spirits. I might die later from
Parsons' damnable poison, but I want to know I beat him.
If only for a short while, I want to know I outfoxed that
son of a bitch!"

Red spots came to her pale cheeks. Slocum would not

have thought a nude woman could show so much fire, so much dignity, so much determination all at once. Yvette did. And that pleased him more than anything they had done together.

"A promise," he said. "I know where Parsons mixes up his devil's brew. There must be some stashed there." Slocum was lying through his teeth now, but he had an idea how to make the antidote after watching what Parson had done.

"I'll hold you to it," Yvette said, going on tiptoe to kiss him lightly again. Then she moved from him and looked down at her nakedness, as if noticing it for the first time. "I need some clothes."

Slocum considered taking them from the deputy, but the man was short and squat, and his clothes would flap loosely on Yvette. That would not attract as much attention as her naked body, but Slocum wanted to avoid anyone noticing her if she was to help with the jailbreak. Together they searched the stables and found old clothing that fit her better, if not well.

"What's your plan to get Baker free?" she asked.

That was a poser. Slocum had none.

"Webber is going to hang Baker come sundown tomorrow," Slocum said. He looked up, saw sunlight slanting down through cracks in the livery walls, and realized more time had passed than he thought. It was already "tomorrow" and Parsons might ask for Baker to swing at any time. The undertaker had seemed eager to bury Caswell. Since Slocum knew how Parsons and his ghoulish wife celebrated mass burials, he wanted to avoid the cemetery at all costs.

"Sometimes Parsons likes a noonday hanging," she said. "It just got so hot he went to evenings, after the sun set."

"You'll need a horse. We need one for Baker too." He looked at the sorrel he had stolen. The horse munched contentedly enough on the hay remaining in the stable.

"Where will we go when we get Baker free?" she asked.

Before Slocum could answer, he heard men outside the

stable. Slocum pressed his finger to Yvette's lips and
pointed. She nodded that she understood. They led the sorrel out the side as Marshal Webber and two deputies came
in through the main doors.

"We've got to move quick," Slocum said. "Can you steal
a horse on your own?"

"That's a hanging offense," Yvette said, grinning crookedly. "As if I care now!"

"Remember," Slocum said. "I promised to get you out
of Lost Soul."

"I trust you, John." Yvette blew him a kiss and said, "I'll
create a diversion. You get Baker out. Where do we meet?"

Slocum gave her the best directions he could to Parsons's
cabin, then finished, saying, "If you can't get away, hide
out and I'll come back for you."

"I know," she said. With that, the blond woman hurried
off. Slocum knew he had little time left. Webber was poking around inside the barn, and soon enough would get the
truth out of the tied-up deputy. The marshal was no man's
fool and would realize what Slocum intended.

Climbing into the saddle, Slocum went directly for the
jailhouse. With the marshal and several deputies otherwise
engaged, this might be the best chance he would have to
rescue Silas Baker. As he rode to the *juzgado,* Slocum saw
the triple nooses twirling slowly in the hot morning wind
whipping off the valley. It took no imagination to picture
himself in the middle, a hemp necktie around his throat,
with Baker on one side and Yvette on the other.

Slocum rode to the side of the jailhouse and dismounted.
Another horse was already tethered here. That would do for
Baker. Yvette was on her own, but Slocum knew that she
was capable. Left to her own devices, she might have even
figured out a way to escape Parsons and his wife by herself.
The undertaker ruled Lost Soul with fear and contempt for
the townsfolk. That was the unholy combination that would
be his downfall.

Slocum had started around the jail when he heard the

front door slam and a heavy locking bar drop into place. He cursed his bad luck. The deputies inside had decided to play it safe. He had no way of battering down the door, and the thick adobe walls would withstand a siege.

As he began to despair of rescuing Baker, Yvette launched her diversion. She set fire to the town, or so it seemed to Slocum. Huge sheets of flame leapt skyward, blocking off his view of the main street. The heat drove him back around the side of the jail—and it drove the deputies out from inside.

The front door slammed open and four men rushed out, screaming in fear. Slocum appreciated their fright. If he had not promised to rescue Baker, he would never have gone into the building. Yvette's fire had consumed the building next to the jail, sending torrents of fiery tarpaper and wood cascading onto the jail roof. The entire structure would burn to a husk in minutes.

Slocum found the keys on the marshal's desk and fumbled, getting into the cell block. Four men shouted at him as he raced to the rear and opened Baker's cell first.

"God, Slocum, you came! Why'd you have to burn the place down around my ears?"

"No time to listen to you grouse," Slocum said. He ripped half the keys off the ring and thrust them into Baker's hands. "Get to work. Let the others out of their cells."

Slocum tried key after key himself until he had freed two of the men. They ran out, not bothering to thank him. That was all right. He had not expected any gratitude. If they turned their anger toward Uriah Parsons, that would be reward enough for Slocum.

"Got 'em," Baker said, finally freeing the other two. The man threw up his arm to shield his face from the blast-furnace heat of the burning roof. Supporting timbers charred through and crashed into the jail, sending sparks and burning fireflies of straw and wood everywhere.

Slocum ducked and dodged until he got free. The heat blistered his back.

"This way, come on!" he shouted to Baker. Slocum rounded the jail in time to see two of the men he had freed mounting the horses, intending to ride away.

Slocum never hesitated. His six-shooter came out in a smooth movement, and he fired twice. At this range, it was hard to miss. He shot both men from their saddles.

"The Lord giveth, the Lord taketh away," muttered Baker, hesitating before he mounted. Slocum impatiently gestured, and Baker got onto the horse, ignoring the spot of blood left by the former rider.

"Where are you?" grumbled Slocum, wheeling the sorrel around in a tight circle as he hunted for any sign of Yvette. The horse began rearing, reacting badly to the fire, the noise, and the heat. Slocum struggled to keep the horse under control.

"What are we waiting for, Slocum? Let's get the hell out of here, unless you want to hang alongside me this afternoon." Baker pointed in the direction of the triple gallows. "Or maybe not."

Slocum noticed that the wood gallows had caught fire and burned merrily. He did not doubt Yvette had single-mindedly set fire to it after torching the building next to the jail. The entire town might go up in flames unless a stroke of luck saved the tinder-dry buildings. Slocum did not see the loss of Lost Soul as that important.

"A friend helped get you out. I want to find—"

Slocum's explanation was cut off by a bullet sailing past his head. The unexpected shot caused his sorrel to rear and startled him. No one in Lost Soul carried a gun. Then Slocum saw the explanation. Parsons had summoned the outriders patrolling the Valley of Spirits. Three armed men pointed their six-shooters in Slocum's direction, alternately firing and shying from the intense heat from the fire. If those men ever got around the barrier formed by the blazing buildings, he and Baker would have a real fight on their hands.

"Slocum!" shouted Baker. "What are you going to do?"

"Ride!" he answered. Yvette had shown spunk. She could get away from Lost Soul and find the shack at the edge of the valley.

And if she didn't, Slocum would come back for her when he could.

He had promised.

16

"Where did those yahoos get guns?" grumbled Baker, his head down as he rode. "The only ones I ever saw wearing iron rode out in the valley, not in the town."

"I reckon that Parsons is getting desperate," Slocum said, distracted. The undertaker had to feel he was losing his absolute control over Lost Soul. He had lost a prisoner sentenced to hang, he'd had half the town burned down around his ears, and maybe worst of all, he could no longer control Slocum. If any one of those things had happened, Parsons might have shrugged it off. All three meant he was headed for disaster. Let the citizens of Lost Soul turn on him and he was as dead as any of the corpses he had planted out in the town cemetery.

Slocum knew Uriah Parsons would not enjoy that trip to the boneyard at all. Even as that thought ran through his head, Slocum also knew that Uriah Parsons's death would mean nothing at all to Purity Parsons. If anything, she *might* celebrate in the same fashion she had before during the mass burial.

"You're lookin' spooked, Slocum. What's eating at you? Other than the obvious?"

Slocum reined back and slowed their pace because his horse began to tire. Running it to death meant his death.

155

"Damned near everything in the Valley of Spirits bothers me," Slocum said. He stood in the stirrups and craned his neck, studying their backtrail. He'd expected to see a posse of armed, angry men on their trail. Not even a hint of dust kicked up by flying hooves showed. Yet. Slocum knew better than to expect a clean getaway.

After all, where was there to escape to? It might be that Parsons's gunmen were biding their time, intending to get him and Baker away from town where killing them would be easier. Something else gnawed at Slocum: Yvette. Had she escaped? Setting a fire as diversion had been dangerous, but it had worked. But if she had been seen and captured by Parsons, the amount of anguish that could be delivered onto her head might make Apache torture seem merciful.

"You had somebody help get me out of jail, didn't you?" asked Baker.

"You talk too much," Slocum said. Like most confidence men, Baker had more than normal insight into what made others tick, and willingly played on anything that looked like weakness or concern.

"I'm not riling you on purpose, Slocum. I want to thank you for breakin' me out. They would've strung me up for sure. I felt the hot breath of the Devil himself on my neck."

"Tell me about getting out of this valley," Slocum demanded. "There's no way we can get back up the canyon. Parsons has guards. Get past them and you run into a war party of Arapahos wanting to take your scalp."

"Didn't know much about them," Silas Baker said, "but the guards made their presence known straightaway. I decided to ride the entire rim around the valley to find another way out. Gave me quite an eyeful."

"The silver mine and all the rest," Slocum said, anxious for the backshooting swindler to get on with it.

"Even a smelter. Never saw men die so quick as in that silver smelter. Parsons goes through men like some folks go through steak and eggs for breakfast. Faster."

"Go on," Slocum said, picking up the pace again. He

considered doubling back on their trail and laying a trap for the men he knew had to be hunting them by now. Parsons would be fit to be tied and might up the ante on the reward. A hundred dollars a head. A hundred ounces of silver. A hundred pounds of silver. Parsons had the wealth to burn.

"You know about the mine shaft. The one leadin' through the mountain. You said as much," Baker said. Slocum nodded, distracted by worrying over hiding their trail. "I never made it through or I'd be out of here, yes, sir, but it goes through. There was plenty of evidence."

"I tried to get through. The place is a maze of cave-ins."

"I had plenty of time to ponder this very topic sittin' in that cell, worryin' about my fate, thinkin' how I would hightail it given half a chance. You gave me that chance. I owe you passage out of here, Slocum. I'm sincere."

Silas Baker had never been sincere a day in his life. Slocum dismissed the promise, but knew he had to hold the man to finding the way through. He had tried and gotten so lost in the mine tunnels that he was hesitant about trying again without some definite plan.

"There a map of the mine tunnels?" Slocum asked.

"Might be," Baker said, turning sly.

Slocum would have beaten the information out of Baker, but he saw the telltale evidence of pursuit on the horizon. It might have been nothing more than a dust devil dancing its lonely way across the dry land, but he did not think so. He wheeled his horse at a sharp angle to the trail they followed and headed for a rise a quarter mile off. Slocum heard Baker calling after him. The man had not spotted the riders yet and protested this detour.

Only after they reached the relative safety of the hillock summit did Slocum bother to point out the riders after them. He touched the six-shooter in its holster and knew he lacked the firepower to hold off even a pair of gunmen. He longed for his Winchester, now long gone, or even saddlebags filled with ammunition for his trusty Colt Navy. All he had was riding in the cylinder. Four shots. No more.

"We can't shoot it out with them," Slocum said. "That means we have to outwit them."

"I'm up for it. How about you, Slocum?" Silas Baker grinned, and Slocum could almost like him in that instant.

They made a quick plan. To Slocum's surprise, Baker did not argue about being used as bait. The man rode off, whistling a jaunty tune, leaving Slocum behind on the hill. Slocum chewed at his lower lip, wondering if he could pull off such an audacious plan. He had no idea how many gunmen they faced.

It might be one too many for him. But he had no choice but to try. If they did not get away from Parsons's hired killers, he could never get back to Lost Soul to see if Yvette had made it through the fire. Then he forgot all about the blonde and her plight and concentrated on the three men coming fast, kicking up a whirlwind of dust and looking mean as hell.

They were determined. So was John Slocum. He took the rope dangling at the side of his saddle, formed a decent loop, and whirled it around a few times, getting the feel of the lariat. Every hunk of hemp spun differently, depending on how wet it was, how old, a dozen other factors. When he thought he could handle the rope with enough skill to make it useful, he set off down the back of the hill, circling to come up behind the three gunmen hot after Silas Baker.

Gunfire told Slocum he had to hurry. He urged his horse on, got the men in sight, and then approached slowly. He wondered what tall tale Baker was spinning for the trio of men with their six-guns leveled on him. Whatever he said, he held their complete attention. Slocum took a settling breath, tightened his knees on the horse, and used his spurs to get the horse galloping forward. All pretense of sneaking up on them vanished when they swung around.

"Yeee-ha!" Slocum shouted as he let fly his lariat. The loop dropped over the shoulders of the middle rider. With an expert jerk, Slocum pulled the rider out of the saddle, dragging the gunman into his partner on the right. The two tumbled to the ground.

A bullet cut through Slocum's shirt, leaving behind pain and a bloody trail when the third gunman reacted instinctively. Slocum yanked back on the reins and his horse dug in heels, kicking up dirt in a low, low spray. A second bullet tore past. And then a dull thud sounded.

Slocum twisted around and saw Baker had acted as fast as he could, jumping the shooter trying to plug Slocum. Baker stood over the fallen man, his fist cocked back for another punch. It was not needed.

"We got ourselves some guns now," Slocum said, picking up the fallen six-shooters from the two men he had roped and knocked to the ground. He leveled one of their own six-guns at them. From the corner of his eye he saw Baker had a gun of his own now.

Slocum was not sure if he trusted Baker with a six-shooter, but the man did nothing to shoot him in the back—again.

"What do we do with them, Slocum?" Baker fingered the trigger, as if he wanted to gun them down in cold blood. Slocum knew he was capable of it, but in spite of all Parsons had done, Slocum saw no reason to kill these men.

"We got their horses. We have their guns. Let's take their boots and tie them up. That ought to put them out of the fight long enough."

"Long enough for what?" sneered the gunman Baker had knocked to the ground. "Parsons will get you for sure. And if you don't drink more of the antidote, you're dead anyhow."

"I've been thinking about that," Slocum said. "I have a way out since I know where he mixes up the brew."

The man looked surprised and then flustered. Finally, regaining his bravado, he shot back, "Parsons has got the blonde. He made her talk. He knows she helped you! She'll die without the blue elixir. He'll make sure she does."

"All the more reason to kill you outright," Slocum said.

"Shut yer pie hole, Davey," growled another of their prisoners. "Yer gonna make him *shoot* us, not let us go."

"Ransom!" cried Davey. "You kin swap us for the woman."

"Do you think Parsons would have anything to do with a trade like that?" Slocum laughed harshly. "He doesn't care spit for you gents. Fact is, he'd love to see you planted six feet under. That's his only pleasure in life, planting dead men."

Slocum saw he had hit the bull's-eye. The three exchanged frightened looks, then lapsed into sullen silence. He had the feeling that if he let them go, they might turn on Parsons.

He took Baker aside and said, "They're no trouble for us. Fact is, we might have allies if they haven't been given the poison."

"Parsons would never give any man a gun who could use it to steal the antidote," Baker said. Slocum believed him. Silas Baker had a swindler's sensibilities and what he said rang true. Parsons would hold men like these three with money, not fear.

"Take their boots and let's ride," Slocum said, anxious to reach the shack. The sooner he got there, the sooner he could find the ingredients that went into the blue antidote, mix it, and dispense it to Yvette and the others in Lost Soul.

"I'm rarin' to get out of the valley too," Baker said.

In less than ten minutes, they rode on, three spare horses trotting along behind. Better, Slocum had two six-shooters stuck into his belt, but it still made him uncomfortable that Baker had a six-gun also. The man had done nothing to make him suspicious of his motives since escaping the jail, but Slocum had not chased him halfway across Nevada to make a mistake now about the man's true character.

Once bitten, twice shy. And he had been bitten good by Silas Baker.

"There it is," cried Baker after they had ridden for more than an hour. He pointed. Sure as sunshine, the ramshackle cabin with the mine tunnel behind it came into view as they topped a rise. Slocum heaved a sigh of relief. From the look of the place, no one had been there since he had left to return to Lost Soul.

They rode down, found a spot where their horses could graze, then went to the cabin. Slocum hesitated, watching Baker closely. The man seemed not to know what was inside the shack.

"You see this place before?" Slocum asked.

"Only from outside. Why?"

"We split anything inside," Slocum said, knowing there was more silver there than a dozen men could haul off. "You take all you want."

Baker frowned, went to the door, and opened it. Slocum wished he could have had a photograph of the man's face when he spotted the wall of silver bars.

"Glory be, I never thought there was that much silver in the world to steal. And here it is, all ours for the takin'!" Baker turned to see if Slocum agreed.

"It's yours—ours," Slocum said.

"Partners!" Baker thrust out his hand. Slocum was slow to take it, knowing how it obligated him. But he did shake Silas Baker's hand in silent agreement that they were bound together by a thread of honor now, even if Slocum could not forget the way the man had robbed him and backshot him in Virginia City.

Baker read Slocum's reluctance and quickly said, "I surely do feel bad about what I done to you, Slocum. That's behind us now. You been nothin' but straight with me, and I'll do the same for you. Honest." Baker made a crossing motion with his finger over his heart.

"Get on into the mine and find the way through to the other side of the mountain. None of this will do us any good if we can't get away."

Slocum saw the cloud pass over Baker's face.

"You *do* know the way out of here?"

"Well, Slocum, like I said, I spent a powerful lot of time

thinkin' on it. I don't *know* the way, not for certain, but think I can find it. Let me get to it." Baker started up the slope toward the mine shaft, then turned and grinned winningly. "Now don't you go takin' *all* the silver while I'm huntin'."

"I have other things to do," Slocum said, amused in spite of himself. Baker waved and vanished into the mine, leaving Slocum to his own devices. Slocum heaved a sigh and went into the cabin. He poked about the shelves along the wall opposite the one of silver ingots and found a small flask of the bright red poison. He swirled it around, watching the way it spun. Cautiously sniffing it caused him to recoil.

Slocum was not sure what was in the red liquid, but it carried a potent odor that lingered like a mad skunk. He put down the flask and hunted for any of the blue elixir that served as an antidote. With enough of it, he could get Yvette out of the Valley of Spirits and to another town where some chemist might figure out what was in the remedy.

The makings Slocum had seen go into the blue fluid were scattered haphazardly along the table, except for brown envelopes of the grainy white powder. Slocum rummaged around, hunting for the powder, thinking it was the essential part of the antidote. He was so engrossed in his hunt for it that he did not hear the cabin door open.

The gust of hot wind from outside was his first hint something was wrong. He turned, saying, "Did you find the way, Baker?"

Slocum froze when he stared down the barrel of a six-shooter held firmly in Purity Parsons's hand.

"Thought you varmints might head here," Purity Parsons said in her cracked voice. She moved into the cabin, the pistol never veering off its target of Slocum's heart.

"What now? You going to shoot me?" Slocum asked. The woman was a cold killer. He had seen that earlier, back in Lost Soul. Whatever milk of human kindness a woman might have was completely missing in this husk of a human being. He kept himself from shuddering as he remembered what she had forced Yvette to do—and he could not bear the thought of what Purity and her husband had done in the cemetery. Some things were too vile to contemplate, even in a world as deadly as John Slocum's.

"I could have plugged you the instant I walked in. No, my handsome young thing, I don't want to kill you. I want something more from you."

Slocum considered throwing down on the woman, no matter that she had the drop on him. Better to die cleanly with a bullet in the gut than to give in to her lecherous demands.

"You and me, we can team up," she said. "Be partners. We can share all this silver. Uriah's put up a passel of the silver, ain't he?"

The way the woman spoke, she made it sound obscene. Slocum knew there had to be more to it. No one offered up such wealth for nothing in return.

"I read you like a book," Purity said, leering. "You want to know what it'll take to have me. Me and the silver. Well, pretty boy, it's real simple. Kill Uriah."

"What?" This startled Slocum. He would kill Uriah Parsons for nothing.

"I'm tired of the stupid oaf. He hardly pays any attention to me, mooning over that blond hussy. Besides, he's let power go to his head. He won't leave Lost Soul until the last hombre's dead and buried."

"He surely enjoys the burying part," Slocum said dryly.

"I do too, but Uriah's going too far with it. We got to take our due and get the hell out of this valley."

Slocum hardly believed his ears. Purity Parsons spoke of her "due" and killing off all the people in an entire town for the sheer thrill of it. And she would murder her husband—or have someone else do it—because she was tired of him. Slocum had stepped on black widow spiders with more virtue.

"Who invented the poison he uses to keep the townsfolk in line?" Slocum asked.

"That was Uriah's idea. Now and again, he can come up with something good. But I don't want to talk of that. You'll kill him for me, boy?"

"I'd sooner walk barefoot across ground glass," Slocum said, knowing the consequences. Her hand never twitched. Purity Parsons held the six-gun firmly and expertly.

"You don't want to throw away a future with me, do you? Silver, me, it can all be yours."

She read the answer in his expression about the same time he read the determination in hers to shoot. Slocum tensed, intending to dive out of the way and try to get his own hog-leg unlimbered to return fire, no matter how unlikely it was he would survive.

Purity Parsons fired.

17

Slocum moved with incredible slowness, as if his entire world had been dropped into a vat of molasses. He saw Purity Parsons squeezing the trigger. He saw the puff of white smoke from the muzzle. He heard the angry whine of the slug as it ripped past his ear—off target because Silas Baker had come up behind the woman and grabbed her gun hand as she fired.

"There, there, Miz Parsons," cooed Baker, twisting savagely to pull the six-shooter from her grip. "You don't want to play with things that might go hurtin' anybody, now do ya?"

"You, you!" Purity Parsons sputtered as her anger grew at having been thwarted in killing Slocum. She fought in Baker's grip, but the man held her tightly.

"What do we do with a hellion like this, Slocum?" he asked. "She came to the cell quite a few times, she did. Always tauntin' me with stories of how I was to be buried in the potter's field outside Lost Soul. A lost soul, she called me then. What do you have to say now?"

Purity Parsons cussed a blue streak, kicking and trying to bite Baker. Slocum considered his narrow escape and how Baker had saved his life. Then he glared at the woman and knew what he had to do. Turning, he scooped up the glass bottle with the red liquid—the deadly poison—in it.

"Hold her," Slocum said, advancing. Purity's eyes widened in surprise when she saw what he intended.

"You miserable cur. You—"

Baker grabbed her chin and forced her mouth open so Slocum could pour in the blood-red poison. The liquid dribbled down her chin as she choked, but enough went down her throat to match the amount Slocum had seen Uriah Parsons force on Yvette.

"Let her go," Slocum said. "She . . ." His voice trailed off when he saw the expression that passed ever so fleetingly across the woman's ugly face.

"You killed me! I need the antidote or I'll die now!" she cried.

Slocum looked at the bottle in his hand. A few drops of the fluid remained. He looked at Purity Parsons, then drank the poison himself. He made a face. A biting, peppery taste tore at his tongue and throat. But he saw no triumph on Purity Parsons's face.

"This stuff is harmless," he said, realizing the extent of the incredible fraud the undertaker and his wife had perpetrated on the people of Lost Soul. "You made them think it was poison, but it is just lousy-tasting colored water."

"You don't know that," she accused.

"I know it," Slocum assured her. The expression that had passed over her was one of triumph and arrogance at having fooled him. There had been nothing but feigned fear. "Pepper. There is a passel of black pepper in it," he said, looking around the cabin. He had thought Parsons's taste ran to spicy food. Now he knew otherwise. Some kind of coloring, maybe iodine and something else to give the maroon color.

"Wait a minute, Slocum," said Baker. "You mean to tell me these two owlhoots have got the whole danged town by the balls with nothin' more than a *fake* poison?" Baker scratched his head. "I surely do admire the audacity. That's 'bout the greatest hoax I ever heard."

Slocum started to warn Baker to keep up his guard, but he was too late. Purity Parsons kicked out and connected with Baker's knee, causing his leg to buckle. As he went down in a pile, the woman dove for the gun he had dropped. Slocum whipped out his six-shooter and aimed it, but hesitated for fear of shooting Baker.

This small faltering allowed Purity Parsons to scoop up the gun and turn it on him. He froze, hand on his ebony handled six-gun.

"I got you now, pretty boy. We coulda been partners, in bed and out. You'll never know what you passed up, 'cuz you're passing on right now!"

Again Silas Baker saved Slocum's bacon. The swindler whirled about like a top of the floor, his legs tangling Purity's. She fell heavily and Baker scrambled for the gun. The report filled the tiny cabin. Baker's body crashed against the woman, pinning her to the floor, giving Slocum time to get his own smoke wagon out and rolling. The second report was as deadly as the first. He killed Purity Parsons with a single bullet to the head.

Silas Baker flopped over, moaned, and lay still. Slocum knelt beside him and tried to make him more comfortable. The bullet from Purity's six-shooter had ripped through the man's chest, leaving a gaping hole that gushed blood. Something was torn up bad inside.

"That's twice you saved me," Slocum said. "Thanks."

Baker's eyelids fluttered and a tiny smile crept onto his face. Then he turned his eyes uphill, toward the mine. The fingers on his right hand twitched, three, then one, and then he switched to his left hand and waved all five. Then he sank back. Slocum thought he died with a smile and the word "partner" on his lips.

Dying quick was about all any man could expect, that and a decent funeral. Slocum spent an hour digging in the hard, rocky ground to make a suitable grave for Silas Baker. He finished his chore and looked at the mounded rocks on the body.

"Who'd've thought it would end like this?" Slocum said. He considered saying some words, but nothing seemed appropriate except, "Partner."

He did not go to any such trouble for Purity Parsons. He lugged her body out into the hot sun fifty yards from the cabin and left it for the buzzards. Even so, he felt this was more than she deserved. At least some good would come from her death, if feeding carrion birds was a good deed.

Slocum went back into the cabin and stared at the wall of silver. He heaved a sigh. He ought to load it into the ore cart in the mine and start hunting for a way through to the other side of the mountain. Parsons went through. There had to be a way. Baker had thought so. And so did Slocum. But he had other obligations to tend to first.

Turning to the table littered with the stuff of the bogus poison and its equally fake antidote, Slocum filled a huge glass jar with water from a jug, mixed in chemicals until he got a blue even more vivid than Parsons's, then tossed in whatever he could find to make the concoction taste foul. He was no chemist, but the result looked real enough—as real as Parsons's brew. Slocum shook it up, and then made a second large jar of the brew, not caring if it had the same flavor. He put both jars into burlap bags, went outside, and slung them over the rump of the horse Baker had escaped Lost Soul on. Then Slocum mounted his sorrel and headed back to town.

This time he was loaded for bear, having pistols galore thrust into his belt reminiscent of the days when he had ridden with Quantrill.

Slocum rode into Lost Soul from the south, slowly and looking for trouble. He wanted Marshal Webber and his deputies to come out and try to arrest him. He wanted some of the hired guns Parsons had patrolling the rest of the valley to try to bushwhack him. He was ready for anything.

Anything but what he found. The stench of burned wood bit at his nose. Yvette's diversion had wiped out half the buildings in town, the fire stopping short of the Prairie Dog Saloon. Slocum saw a few faces furtively look from the dirty saloon windows, and figured this was the only place where the townsfolk could assemble now. He dismounted in front of the saloon, got his bags of blue liquid, and carried them in over his shoulder.

Slocum looked around, and knew his guess had been a bull's-eye. Two dozen men huddled together in the bar, not sure what to do.

"Where's Yvette?" Slocum asked. A murmur passed through the crowd, but no one volunteered the information. "What about the marshal?"

"Dead," said the barkeep. "He got burned up in the fire along with half his deputies. The other half, well, we don't know where they've gone. They vanished and no one's asking after them."

Slocum went to the bar and put the heavy jars down. "Whiskey. A bottle of it," he ordered. The barkeep did not bother asking for money. Lost Soul was past that. It was dead or dying and everyone in town knew that, because they were in the same condition.

Slocum drank slowly, aware of eyes fixed on him. When he had downed his second shot of rye, he turned and put his elbows on the bar. They stared at the guns thrust into his gunbelt since it had been a spell since anyone had carried a single six-shooter here, much less four.

"What about Parsons?" said Slocum. "I want that son of a bitch's head."

"Don't know where to find him either," said the barkeep nervously. "We all need to find him ourselves. He . . . he—"

"The lying bastard's got your antidote, is that it?" demanded Slocum.

"We'll die. We'll all die, just like Caswell and the others if we don't get it. We can't let you harm him. You hurt him and we're all goners," said the barkeep, the only man in the place with spine enough to talk to Slocum.

"You think you can stop me?" asked Slocum. He laid two pistols on the bar.

The barkeep eyed them, licked his dried lips, and shook his head. "We ain't gunfighters, not like you. But we'll do what we have to if it keeps us alive one more day. We seen how awful men die if they can't get their antidote in a timely fashion."

Slocum did not move a muscle. He stared into the barkeep's eyes. He saw a slow change in the man's expression; then curiosity built and finally the bartender had to ask, "What'd you mean callin' Mr. Parsons a liar?"

"Just that," Slocum said. "He controls you by doling out the blue liquid remedy for poison he forced on you, but he never told you a deep, dark secret."

"What might that be?" said a man who had been watching silently. "You tellin' us you know somethin' we don't?"

"If you drink twice as much of the blue liquid as Parsons dished out for you last time, it'll eliminate the poison entirely. You'll never have to have another drop of the antidote the rest of your long, natural lives."

"You're lyin'," the man growled. "How do you know that?"

"Because I found where he mixed the devil's brew and read his notes."

"You're lying!" went up the cry.

"Does this look like I'm lying?" Slocum pulled away the burlap bags and showed the two large jars of the blue liquid he had concocted. His hand moved like lightning, yanking one of the six-guns off the bar and aiming it at the crowd. "Stay back."

"You takin' over, is that it?" asked the barkeep. He looked from the jars to Slocum and back. "Whatever you say, we'll do. I think I'm speaking for everyone here."

"I don't want to take over. I want to free you. Everyone," Slocum shouted. "There's enough for you all, but you only need to drink twice what Parsons allotted you the last time. No more. Make sure it all goes around."

The barkeep slid shot glasses down the bar. Men eagerly took two, three, and even four shots, made wry faces at the foul taste, then moved out of the way for the next to imbibe. Slocum presided over the solemn ceremony, seeing that he was freeing them from unholy, nonexistent bonds.

"Why you doing this for us?" asked one man. "We never done nothin' but bring you trouble."

"What's the best way of getting back at Uriah Parsons?" Slocum asked. The man nodded knowingly. Take everything Parsons held dear and destroy it. That was true revenge.

And Slocum would have the sweetest revenge of all when he found Yvette and freed her from the ghoul's depraved grip.

About half a jar remained by the time the last man had sampled Slocum's mixture.

"Save it for anyone else who might need it," Slocum told the barkeep. Then he slid one six-shooter to the man. "Keep this too. You might need it. Anyone else know how to use a six-shooter?" Two hesitant hands went up, as if they were not sure of his intentions. Slocum tossed each of them a six-shooter. "Be sure what you're shooting at," he warned them.

"What if we get that sidewinder Parsons in our sights?" asked one.

"Don't shoot him. He's mine." With that Slocum left the bar. As he stepped into Lost Soul's main street a cheer went up behind him. For the first time it sounded like a saloon inside, men laughing and joking and enjoying themselves. Even the piano sounded more chipper when someone began banging out a tune.

Slocum settled his Colt Navy in its holster and headed for the funeral parlor down the street. The building had escaped destruction, an oasis in a desert of charred structures. He sniffed a few times as the burned smell assaulted his nose, but his concentration never wavered from the funeral parlor's front door. With a tracker's instincts, Slocum knew Uriah Parsons was inside.

It was fitting. A man who lived by death was going to die in the place he felt most secure.

Slocum hesitated at the front doors. Yvette might be prisoner inside. Caution could pay off now, patience and a waiting game.

Slocum threw caution to the hot desert wind and kicked open the door. He bellowed, "Get your ass out here, Parsons, so I can shoot you!"

From the viewing room toward the rear of the funeral parlor came odd snuffling noises, as if a giant rat worked on a hunk of meat. Slocum glanced left and right to be sure he wasn't shot in a cross fire, then pushed aside the curtains to the rear room.

Like some demented animal, Parsons crouched on a coffin, nibbling at something Slocum chose not to dwell on.

"Where's Yvette?" Slocum asked.

Parsons turned mad eyes toward Slocum. He cackled and then tossed aside the well-gnawed bone before jumping to the floor.

"She's a tasty one, she is," Parsons said. "Love to eat her up. Yum, yum!"

Slocum struck Parsons, sending the man rolling like a ball. The undertaker crashed into the far wall and came to his feet, nose bleeding. He paid the minor injury no heed.

"Where are all my slaves? Fools, they are all fools! I know a secret they don't. Do you want me to tell you? Well, I won't!"

"There isn't any poison. There was no need for them to take an antidote," Slocum said coldly, seeing that his enemy had gone completely insane. The fiery, wild light in Parsons's eyes told the story. He had been pushed over the edge of madness when his town burned down and he had lost control.

"What? You lie!"

"I told the people if they drank enough of your blue

mixture, they'd be cured. No one needs you now, Parsons. You're finished. And I found your stash of silver. I'm taking that too."

"No, no, you can't. I won't let you!"

Slocum's hand was a blur as it gripped the ebony handle of his Colt Navy, drew, and fanned three shots into Parsons. The undertaker had grabbed for a long-bladed knife, its handle still gory from his last victim's blood. Slocum watched the undertaker fold into himself, crumple to the floor, and lay utterly still.

In less than a heartbeat, the scourge of Lost Soul had been vanquished. Somehow, Slocum felt no triumph gunning down a man who had become as crazy as a bedbug.

18

Slocum poked around in the funeral parlor hunting for some clue as to Yvette's whereabouts, but found nothing. He even looked into the coffins, fearing Parsons might have killed her and committed his favorite act with her. But none of the bodies was the lovely blonde's.

Slocum had started out the front door when he found himself facing a half-dozen men, all with six-shooters slung at their sides. He recognized one as having been Parsons's hired gunman, one fresh from guarding the canyon leading out of the Valley of Spirits. Slocum turned slightly to get a better angle when the shooting began.

He was surprised when the man held up his hands, palms outward, and said, "Wait! There's no need to go gettin' antsy. We come to settle accounts, but from the smell of gunsmoke in there, I reckon you already done that."

"Parsons is dead," Slocum said, waiting for a reaction. A look of relief crossed the man's weather-beaten face.

"Thanks," was all he said. The man gestured, and the others with him retreated to their horses across the street. Slocum figured the men Parsons had hired were getting out while the getting was good. If townspeople started showing up with guns, that meant some of them might get killed— something Parsons had never paid them for. They had been

175

set to bottle up anyone brave enough to attempt to escape the Valley of Spirits. Uriah Parsons had taken care of the chance of anyone shooting at them by preventing any in town from carrying a gun.

At least he had until John Slocum showed up.

The gunmen rode from Lost Soul in a tight knot, as if closeness could get them through the canyon leading away from town and the valley. For all he knew, this might work. The Arapahos might let an armed, determined band of men through. Somehow, he doubted it. Parsons's hired guns would ride smack into the teeth of the other half of a trap they had helped set.

Slocum looked around the mostly deserted, mostly destroyed town. People stirred sluggishly, as if rising stupefied from a long winter's sleep, and Slocum could not tell what their purpose was. If they had any sense, they'd join up with the armed men and try to escape. Then again, with Parsons and his wife dead, that silver mine could make for a powerful lot of rich men.

All they had to do was get the hell out of the valley now and then swap the plunder for food and essentials. If nothing more, Slocum wanted to give his stolen horse a meal of decent grain and a grooming. But he knew there would be more than tending his horse. Much, much more, with this mountain of silver bars his for the spending.

Slocum walked down the street, his sharp eyes scanning the buildings for any sign of Yvette. He heard her long before he found her huddled in the corner of what remained of Caswell's store. As so many times before, she was hunkered down, knees pulled up and face buried as she cried. Slocum pushed through the wreckage and perched on the burnt corner of the counter, watching her, waiting for her to realize she was no longer alone.

When she looked up, her blue eyes bloodshot, it was in anger.

"You let them have it all!" she cried. Yvette balled her fists and shook them futilely in the air. "You sentenced me to death, after I helped you, after you promised. No antidote and I'll die, I'll die!" Yvette went back to sobbing.

Slocum started to tell her about Parsons and his swindle, then thought better of it. Explaining might not work because Parsons had done such a good job convincing her. Parsons had gotten a stranglehold on everyone's emotions, not their logic. Might be he had put rat poison in some of the red liquor just to make it seem more deadly. Slocum had to fight back the same underhanded way to free Yvette of her nonexistent bonds.

"I promised I'd come back, that I'd get you out, didn't I?"

"Yes, but—"

"I know where Parsons mixed up the antidote. You can drink a gallon of it, if you like, but only a few ounces will remove it completely from your body."

"Y-you're sure?"

"You helped me, you helped get Baker out of jail. I always pay my debts."

"You came back just for me?"

"See me talking to anyone else?"

Yvette struggled to her feet and stumbled over, throwing herself into his arms. "You're lying, all men are liars, but I don't care. Lie to me some more."

"Well," Slocum said, "after we get you cured, I'm going to make you rich. Stinking rich. Richer than you ever thought you could be. Parsons owes you that much, for all he's done to you."

"How are we going to get out of the valley?"

Slocum paused before answering. Baker had been certain a path existed through the maze of mine tunnels, but had died before finding it. Or had he? Slocum frowned as he remembered the last few seconds of Baker's life.

"There's a way out—and not back through the canyon."

"All Parsons' guards are gone. I . . . I saw them leave. But the Indians are still there."

"Still riled at us white eyes riding through their sacred

land, I reckon," Slocum said, surer than ever Parsons had sneaked the silver across the mountains using the ore cart and tunnels in the abandoned mine.

He led Yvette from the burned store and found a horse for her. Together, they rode back to Parsons's cabin at the mouth of the mine.

"What are we going to do, John? You don't know your way through. Neither do I," she said, eyeing the gaping maw of the mine suspiciously.

"First things first," he said. "You rustle up some food for us while I mix the antidote."

"How do you know what went into it?"

"I forced Parsons to give me the formula before he died," Slocum said, lying through his teeth. Yvette appeared skeptical, but wanted to believe he knew what he was doing when he started clanking glassware together and mixing the potion. As he worked, Slocum was aware of Yvette watching him like a snake watches a bird. He moved with confidence, knowing it hardly mattered what he put into the mixture as long as it tasted bad enough to make the woman think it was real.

Sloshing about half a Mason jar full of the blue liquid, he handed it to her.

"Drink twice what Parsons gave you. More is all right, but twice the dose is all you really need."

"He told you?"

"He didn't lie," Slocum said. "He couldn't. Not when I was through with him."

Yvette swallowed, closed her eyes, then tipped back the jar. She drained a quarter of it, choked, and spat some out.

"That's awful!" she cried. "It doesn't taste like the stuff he gave me."

"It is, though," Slocum said, thinking fast. "The difference in taste means it is working, wiping out the poison in your body because you finally drank enough."

"Really?"

Slocum said nothing. She wiped her lips and looked fearfully at him. It was time to get her mind on other things. He pointed to the wall of silver bars.

"How many of those do you want?"

"Want!" she cried. "I'll take 'em all!"

"Don't get greedy," he warned. "I want some. Come on, help me move them to the mine."

Together they toiled, moving a stack of silver ingots and placing them into the ore cart. When the cart was half-filled with a fortune in silver, Slocum reflected on how little they had actually removed from the cabin. The two of them could be richer than Collis P. Huntington if they found the path through the maze of tunnels.

He stopped, scratching his chin, remembering Silas Baker again. The man had been dying and had made strange gestures.

"I got some food and water, John," Yvette said. "Let's get out of this horrid place."

Slocum had to agree. He had spent far too long and seen too much sorrow in the Valley of Spirits. Time to move on and find a place to spend some of the riches in the ore cart. He got behind it and dug in his toes, getting the cart moving. It rolled along the track easily enough once in motion, but Slocum found himself wondering where to go, which of the tunnels to follow. He had gotten lost before and had burned through too many candles, finding more cave-ins than promise of a route to the other side.

As he passed the shelf with the miner's candles, he scooped up a box and dropped it into the cart. Then he picked up the stubs of others in case they needed them. He remembered the flare of panic at the idea he was going to be lost forever in the blackness of the mines. Slocum was not afraid of tight places, but the dark had let his imagination believe the walls had collapsed around him and crushed him.

"Let's hurry, John. I don't like it in here. Which way do we go?" Yvette stood at the first juncture, one right, one ahead, one to the left. Slocum bent down, using a candle to study the tracks. The rust had been knocked off all the rails—or had never really formed. He saw some evidence that many of the rails in the tunnel had been replaced, possibly by Parsons to make the trip through the mine easier as he moved out his treasure.

"John, which way?"

"Straight on," Slocum decided. He had no idea, but felt he needed to sound decisive. As he pushed the cart, he thought of Baker again. The man's hands. The twitching. The way he had looked so intently at Slocum before he died, as if he had tried to tell Slocum something.

What? What did the dead man have to say?

"Look, John, another juncture."

Again Slocum examined the rails, but could not figure out what to do. He started to go down the right tunnel, then stopped dead in his tracks.

"Right three," he muttered.

"What's that?"

"Baker. He thrust out his right hand and showed me three fingers. Three, as if we're supposed to take the third tunnel on the right."

"That's pretty farfetched," Yvette said. "It doesn't sound as if you know where we're going. We're going to be lost in here and die!"

"Quiet," he snapped. "I *don't* know for certain, but I do know men. At the end Baker wouldn't double-cross me. He wouldn't. He saved my life a couple times." Under his breath, Slocum added, "And it might just be a third time."

They took the third tunnel to the right. Almost immediately Slocum was worried that he had chosen poorly. The uphill slope made pushing the cart almost impossible. Then he stepped in dried dung.

"This is the way," he said with renewed certainty. This lent him strength to get to the top of the stope. He stared into the flickering candle and remembered the rest of Baker's silent instructions.

"First right," he said, seeing a tunnel ahead. He pushed

faster. In no time, the cart was going downhill, almost getting away from him. He had to apply the brakes.

"Where, John, where now?" asked a bewildered Yvette. She held the candle over her head and looked at the most curious array of drifts Slocum had ever seen in a mine. Six tunnels ran off in all directions, confusing him further about which direction they were headed.

"Three right, one right, five left," he said, hoping there were no more choices that had to be made. Baker might have died before he could tell of others. Slocum was tired from pushing the ore cart, and had no idea how far they had gone in the underground labyrinth. All he knew was that they had burned through more than six candles.

Slocum engaged Yvette in idle chitchat, more to keep his own mind off the possibility that Parsons might have the last laugh and from his seat in Hell see them buried alive. More than one of the tunnels they passed had caved in. The rattling steel wheels on the tracks might cause weakened sections of mine roof to fall on their heads. Or they might starve or die of thirst. Or . . .

"John, what's that ahead?" Yvette asked.

Slocum laughed with joy and put his back to pushing faster. The cart popped from the mouth of the mine and crashed into a wood stop at the end of the tracks. He took off his hat and let out a rebel yell that could be heard halfway to Georgia.

"We made it!" he cried.

In the distance he saw a town—and it was not Lost Soul. All around showed signs of commerce. A farm a few miles off looked to have lush green pastures, indicating water, possibly from an acequia, maybe from a river running through the area. And in the distance, far, far off, Slocum was certain he saw the curling white plume of steam rising from a locomotive smokestack.

They had reached the far side of the mountain!

"Oh, John, I'm sorry I ever doubted you," Yvette said, hugging him tightly. He laughed, then sobered.

"We have to go back, you know."

"Why?"

"Our horses. I'm not leaving them back in the valley to wander off and graze. I stole them fair and square." Slocum grinned a little more as he went on. "And the silver, of course. I'll be damned if I am going to leave that much silver for anyone else, not when we can spend it just as easily."

Yvette laughed and held onto his arm. She rested her head on his shoulder and said, "I want a bath first. And food. And a soft bed." She turned her face up to his and said, "And I want you."

He looked into the ore cart and knew her wishes would be granted. Together they started down the hill, lugging along a few bars of silver.

Slocum said as they started along the road leading to the bustling town, "There's one thing I want to know."

"What's that?" Yvette asked.

"I never found out what your last name is."

"Does it matter?"

"No," he said, realizing it didn't matter one whit.

LONGARM

Explore the exciting Old West with one of the men who made it wild!